BEWITCHED AVENUE SHUFFLE

BEWITCHED AVENUE SHUFFLE

SCIONS OF MAGIC™ BOOK THREE

TR CAMERON   MICHAEL ANDERLE   MARTHA CARR

DISRUPTIVE IMAGINATION®

Copyright © 2020 TR Cameron & Michael Anderle
Cover Art by Jake @ J Caleb Design
http://jcalebdesign.com / jcalebdesign@gmail.com
Cover copyright © LMBPN Publishing
A Michael Anderle Production

LMBPN Publishing
PMB 196, 2540 South Maryland Pkwy
Las Vegas, NV 89109

First US edition, January, 2020
Version 1.01, February 2020
ebook ISBN: 978-1-64202-675-7
Print ISBN: 978-1-64202-676-4

Thanks to the JIT Readers

Jeff Goode
Diane L. Smith
Jeff Eaton
Dorothy Lloyd
Dave Hicks
Larry Omans
Deb Mader
Paul Westman

If I've missed anyone, please let me know!

Editor
Skyhunter Editing Team

For those who seek wonder around every corner and in each turning page. And, as always, for Dylan and Laurel.

— TR Cameron

CHAPTER ONE

Caliste Leblanc imagined that any of the New Orleans party crowd who saw the three of them flash past would remember the sight, assuming they weren't too intoxicated. The man they pursued was dressed like Dracula, a result of the decision to confront him at the end of the evening vampire tours. Their quarry had been a part of the Atlantean gang back in the day and was now mostly legit, Tanyith reported after several days of surveillance, although not above a little petty theft when the opportunity presented itself.

She was a step ahead of her partner and made a mental note to tease him about the obvious onset of age-related decay. Her black boots thudded on the sidewalk, and she wore mostly matching hues—jeans and a concert t-shirt with faded lettering promoting The Police, with the cover symbols from *Ghost in the Machine* in a slightly darker black than the rest. Her curly red hair trailed unfettered like the tail of a rocket.

He pounded along a pace behind. She risked a quick

glance at the former prisoner and current amateur wannabe private eye. His chiseled face was filled with annoyance and sweat darkened the armpits of his untucked white dress shirt. *So that's something else to taunt him with.* "Stop that vampire!" he shouted.

A crowd of laughing revelers raised their gigantic beer bottles in a toast as the trio whipped past, and Cali shook her head. *He had to choose to run along Bourbon street, naturally. Even if this group wanted to help, their reflexes are so damaged they'd miss by a block and a half.*

In the week of relative quiet since the events at the docks, Tanyith had investigated all the people he knew from the gang who were still around and no longer an obvious part of the criminal group. His effort was focused on the intention to locate someone who might have information about Sienna's missing boyfriend. Most had nothing to share and welcomed his inquiries with varying degrees of enthusiasm. This one, though, ran as soon as he saw them, which suggested it had been a good call to ask her to accompany him. *Fleeing at the sight of us has to mean something, right?*

Their quarry looked over his shoulder at her partner's shout and hissed, then suddenly surged forward with a burst of speed. *You're taking the whole Nosferatu identity a little far, buddy.*

Cali pulled up a touch of magic—only enough to get the job done—and put her most recent lesson from Emalia to work. Power flowed into her legs to energize them and enable her to run faster. She'd been sad at the revelation that she couldn't become superhero-fast, the top limit being what her body could handle before it actually damaged itself. Still, she was half again as fast with it as she was without it. She narrowed the distance, then growled in annoyance and slid to a stop several yards beyond the archway he'd ducked into to evade her lunge at his cloak.

Tanyith gave her a superior look as he took the corner with ease. She grimaced and moved at normal speed in the right direction in time to see the caped figure dart through the tables of a packed restaurant patio. Diners shrieked, waiters yelled as they dodged or fell, and shouts from the bartender in a language she didn't recognize followed her as she trailed the others. She did her best to avoid colliding with anyone but still stumbled from a chair that she'd mostly, but not entirely, leapt over. When they emerged onto the crowded streets once more, their target was now a fair distance ahead of her, with her partner a dozen paces behind him.

A sensation of a new presence in her mind and a metallic flash overhead heralded the arrival of Fyre, and the Draksa swooped with his claws extended toward the fugitive. A faint shimmer surrounded the creature who'd adopted her, a trace of the veil that rendered him invisible from everyone other than her. He was about to snatch their quarry when the man tumbled into a somersault that allowed him to evade the dragon lizard's sharp grasp. He hurtled through the doorway of an apartment building, which gave Cali flashbacks to the ambush laid for her a couple of weeks before. She gritted her teeth and pursued, confident that if there was a trap ahead, she and Tanyith would be able to deal with it and that Fyre would prevent any outside reinforcements from joining the melee.

She cleared the doorway as she drove her shoulder into

the closing door, burst into the structure, and had a moment of disbelief at what lay within. While the exterior of the building appeared to contain a set of six separate apartments, the interior held only a single large room that stretched three tall stories high and occupied a rectangle about forty feet wide and sixty long. Long strands of twinkling lights adorned the walls, doubtless repurposed from Christmas decorations. Mismatched bunks and sleeping bags, most occupied, covered almost the entire ground level. A part of the area was sectioned off with *shower* scrawled on the plywood that enclosed it in spray paint. Pictures done by graffiti artists filled the first-floor drywall, judging by the style. Some had ventured higher but not so many as to fully cover the other levels. *Or where the other levels would be if the place wasn't gutted.*

The man panted in the center of the room, bent over with one palm raised in a "stop" gesture toward them. Tanyith and Cali obeyed, not because of the signal but because of the two men and two women who trained pistols on them.

Her partner muttered, "Whoa, now. We only want to talk. There's no need to escalate."

One of the men laughed. "I'd say you did the escalating when you apparently chased our friend."

Cali shook her head. "He chose to run. All we wanted was a little conversation. Maybe you could lower those weapons? We wouldn't want one to go off by accident." In truth, they looked experienced enough that she didn't worry about unintended bullets fired inadvertently. Still, it was always preferable to have a weapon barrel pointed somewhere other than at one's face.

The woman with the man who'd spoken, both off to Cali's right, shook her head. "I have a better idea. You and your boyfriend back out of here. Now."

She sighed. "He's not my boyfriend and I'm not an archaeologist." The woman tilted her head as a quizzical expression crept onto her face and she sighed again. "Because archaeologists are into fossils. And I'm not into fossils. Or an archaeologist." She rolled her eyes. "Okay, enough." She raised her fingers to her mouth an inch at a time so as to not set the gun-wielders off and used them to discharge a sharp whistle. Moments later, the surrounding air was disturbed by Fyre's passage. She kept her gaze locked on the woman to avoid betraying his presence.

With her hands on her hips, she noted that the man they'd pursued was now properly upright and breathing normally. *Which means he's able to talk.* "Here's the thing. All we want to do is have a short chat. If you aim the weapons at the floor, we won't have to take them from you. Of course, that means if you don't, we will."

The man laughed derisively and twitched his pistol at her. "I'd like to see you try."

Cali answered with her magic. With a twisting dive to the left, she fired a force blast to knock the weapon out of his hand. In her keyed-up state, she misjudged the power and he careened back and tripped over one of the bunks. *At least I didn't send him through the wall.* A curse from the woman signaled Tanyith dealing with her, the gun, or both. A chill pervaded the air before she rolled up from her dodge. The gun-wielders were frozen in place, and the other people in the room, all of whom were awake now, cringed away from the suddenly visible Draksa.

The man who'd led them there twitched, and she pointed a finger at him. "Don't even think about it, or I'll have him freeze your legs." She and Tanyith walked over to stand before him, and she gestured for her partner to take the initiative.

He stepped forward and shook his head. "All right, Parker, why lead us on this chase? And why the hell are you working as a tour guide? A friend told me you'd cleaned your act up and come into some cash. I don't think this is what she was referring to."

Parker sighed and finger-combed his hair out of his eyes. His locks were floppy, perhaps a sign that he was growing them to better fit his image as a creature of the night. The face below them was clean-shaven and sharply angled, and his slender form was mostly hidden beneath the black and red cape, white shirt, and black trousers. Sneakers ruined the look, but at least they were black. His laugh held portions of disbelief, regret, and resentment. "Tay, it figures you'd be back in town at the precise moment when everything went to hell. You've always been trouble's lackey."

Tanyith frowned. "Let's let bygones be gone, Park. What are you talking about?"

With a suspicious glance at the Draksa, the man took a few steps sideways, sat on a bunk, and folded his hands in his lap. "I had a good thing going with one of the smaller groups in town. We didn't do any of the really bad stuff, only a little smuggling for rich folks—things from the homeland."

"Rich Atlanteans?" Cali interjected.

The man frowned at her with enough condescension

that she considered having Fyre freeze his feet. "No, for humans. There are some who consider themselves collectors of arcane knowledge and artifacts."

"Not actual artifacts, surely." Her partner sounded alarmed. "You're not that stupid, are you?"

The laugh he uttered seemed forced like it had to fight to escape the clutches of his chest. "Sadly, that's a shoe that fits. Our boss had a connection. Then, suddenly, he didn't and we were attacked by the Atlantean gang." He shrugged. "I walked away from everything—a new place, a new ID, and new job, such as it is. The last I saw of the others, they were headed to the swamps."

She looked at her partner and he nodded sharply to verify that the man's words were likely the truth. But something in how he'd said it scratched at her instincts. "Who was the final collector you worked for?"

He shook his head. "I don't know. That was boss-level stuff."

With a scowl, she folded her arms. "There's no way you didn't discuss it among yourselves and try to find out. Spill, or you'll go into deep freeze." She gestured toward Fyre.

Parker glanced at the dragon lizard and sighed. "Rion Grisham."

"It had to be him." Cali put her head in her hands but spoke loudly enough to be heard through her fingers. "And what's the last thing you sourced for him—the thing that pushed it over the edge with the others?" She knew what it had to be even before he answered. Finding the first piece was random chance. Discovering the second among the things her parents left for her pointed to something bigger.

"A hunk of metal with stuff engraved on it. Part of a sword, the boss said, from long ago."

She sighed. "Of course it was."

Tanyith snapped his fingers, and both she and Parker turned to him. "That's all very interesting, but it's tangential. What I really need to know is this—when was the last time you saw Aiden Walsh?"

The man frowned. "Who?"

"You might know him as Adam Harlan or Harry."

Parker laughed. "Oh, that guy. He's an idiot." She noticed the flicker of a smile on her partner's face at the characterization, but it vanished quickly. "Probably about a month ago. He was trying to get in with the boss or something, I guess. They were talking at a bar."

"Which one?"

"I don't remember and it probably wouldn't matter. They didn't, like, simply run into each other. Someone put them together."

Tanyith growled his irritation. "Who?"

The other man shrugged. "I don't know. Not me. But what I can tell you is that one other person was there for that meeting."

"Who was it?"

Parker stood suddenly, and Cali reached inward to touch her magic, ready for anything. He stepped forward to look the other man in the eye. "Something for nothing, is it?"

He shook his head. "You owe me. A number of times over."

"This clears it." It was a statement, not a question, and

he received a nod in response. "Fine. It was Grisham's jerkwad assistant."

She thought back to when Grisham and his associates visited the Dragons to deliver their threats and promises. "The muscle or the brain?" She'd put her money on the thin man, who'd had as much intelligence sparkling in his eyes as his partner had bulges straining the lines of his suit.

The man laughed. "The smart one. I'm not sure the other is capable of speech. But I'll give you this for free since Tay and I are even after so long. Grisham has two smart ones, at least, and maybe more. His fingers are in way more pies than anyone outside his inner circle knows about." His voice turned stern, and the two guards who'd been thawed stepped behind him. "Now, get out. You're not welcome here, ever."

Fyre snarled once, which made the trio flinch visibly, but they relaxed as the team departed without further incident. Once they were back on the street, Cali asked, "Do you feel like we'll never get any useful answers and only more questions?"

Tanyith laughed darkly. "Yes, exactly that." The dragon lizard snorted his agreement.

"Fantastic." Sarcasm dripped from the word as she shook her head. *New week, new troubles. But at least I made good tips tonight. Maybe I'll treat Emalia to lunch tomorrow while I grill her for information on the sword.*

CHAPTER TWO

The decision to sleep in hadn't been entirely voluntary, but after spending the early morning hours racing through the streets, Cali had been grateful for the break. Unfortunately, it meant she was late to meet her great aunt, so not only was there no time to take her out to lunch, but she had to wait outside while Emalia told the fortunes of a tourist couple. The woman's ability to correctly predict the future was remarkable, although most of her customers doubtless attributed her accuracy to coincidence or luck rather than true magic.

Her great-niece knew better. Beyond a shadow of a doubt, her last remaining known relative had the gift. In cultures past, she would have been an adviser to queens, a village's wise woman, or some such thing. While predicting job promotions and finding lost items for tourists was a far cry from those lofty roles, Emalia seemed content with her life. *Well, except where my studies are concerned. Then, it's all "you can do better" and "why do you want to make an old woman sad?"* She laughed quietly and a wave of affection for her teacher and guide swept through her. Not a day went by when she wasn't keenly aware of how lucky she was to have her mentor in her world.

The lock on the door clicked as the couple exited. The man looked stunned and his apparent girlfriend dragged him along as if in a hurry to get somewhere. Cali ducked past them into the shop. The public room was decorated in black and purple fabric and contained a low table with a crystal ball and three seats around it as the only furniture. Emalia sat in one, dressed for work in a long flowing robe with her grey hair piled perfectly atop her head. Sharp eyes tracked her and the Rottweiler at her heels, and a grin spread across her face. "Fyre, Caliste, it's so good of you to visit."

She groaned. The use of her full name was a signal that she'd done something to irk her mentor. The older woman rose at her approach and escorted the new arrivals behind the curtain at the back of the room. Beyond was a small kitchenette, with a well-worn rectangular table in the middle, the yellowing plastic top peeling at the corners. She sat, obedient to Emalia's unwritten rules, and remained quiet until a steaming cup of rejuvenating tea was set before her. Tentatively, she took a sip and grimaced. "I don't think this recipe is a step in the right direction unless your goal is to use it as a punishment."

The older woman sat primly, her posture perfect, and tasted her own beverage. Her lips twisted a little to satisfy the girl's desire that she share in the pain, and she set it down slowly. "What it lacks in taste, it should balance by restoring your magic." Cali had long been concerned with maximizing her pool of power, and only in the last month had she learned that it was because the reservoir had been artificially limited by her parents to keep her existence from registering on her enemies' magical radars. Now, with that restriction removed, she had more than was sufficient. Still, Emalia demonstratively believed it best to ensure it was topped off. The woman's brow lowered as she stared at her student. "You're late."

She pointed at the disguised Draksa curled under the table. "It's his fault." The creature snorted chill breath over her feet, and she shivered. "Okay, it's my fault. I gave Tanyith a hand after work last night and it took longer than expected."

The other woman nodded. "I heard."

Startled, she raised her eyebrows in a question. "You did? Already? How?"

Her teacher laughed. "I have my ways." She lowered her tone and switched to her fortuneteller's role. "The streets have a voice if you only know how to listen, child."

Cali rolled her eyes. "Okay, spooky lady. Whatever." They shared a laugh, and she continued, "Actually, before we do any training, I have to ask you about something."

"It sounds serious." Emalia adopted an expression that was overly attentive, and they both laughed together again.

"Stop. It is serious. What do you know about the broken sword piece my parents left me?"

The corner of her mouth quirked. "I know you should visit the library to research it."

You'd think everyone in my life owned stock in the library given how excited they are about my going there. "It's in my plans as soon as I have a chance. But last night, we learned that Rion Grisham bought a piece of something that sounds identical to it. And we already know the Atlanteans have a similar piece. That's too many to be a coincidence, wouldn't you say?"

Her aunt nodded. "I would agree. I've had a discussion with Invel on that topic, actually."

She wiggled her eyebrows. "It seems like you've found a number of reasons to chat with him lately, Great Aunt." The Drow was a friend of Zeb's and a member of the magical council that collaborated on common issues facing their communities in the Crescent City. He was knowledgeable about a wide variety of things by virtue of his position as a buyer and seller of unusual goods, more often than not magical and frequently of dubious sources.

"Pish." She waved a hand at the suggestion, but the slight curls at the corners of her mouth revealed the truth. *Well, what do you know?* "He is of the opinion that your piece is a portion of an artifact sword, based on the engravings. Presumably, the others are part of the same weapon since it would be odd for there to be multiple versions."

"Odd, but not impossible."

"Of course not. But unlikely."

"So what exactly is an artifact sword?"

Emalia sighed, took another sip of the tea, and winced. "You do really need to go to the library."

Cali laughed. "Why? I have you."

The woman shook her head in mock despair. "An artifact sword has power of some kind infused into it. Many different types exist, and there's no particular way at the moment to identify which this one might be. Some have the ability to store power for you to draw upon. Others have memories trapped within that can share knowledge. There are even those that have the power to heal, or so I've heard. And there are bound to be more than only those. I haven't made a study of it."

"So, in any case, I should probably be concerned that both the human and Atlantean gangs are interested in the sword."

"I think that's a fair statement."

She sighed. "Okay. So, we'll add that to the remaining mysteries of the key, the book, and the other charms."

Her aunt snapped her fingers. "Actually, I've discovered something about the key. Invel recognized a marking on it from the picture I showed him. It's for a commercial building or a storage unit."

That drew a pained groan. "There are how many storage places around New Orleans? I'll never find it."

Her mentor nodded. "That would be a challenge. But I bet you could narrow down other kinds of commercial buildings. There are probably only a few located at a 1601 address anywhere nearby."

Cali considered that, then agreed. "You're right. That's not too bad. I can check that on the Internet after work. But if it turns out to be a storage unit, we'll need an army of volunteers to find the correct one."

"Then let's hope it's not that. Are we done with the questions?" She nodded. "Good, finish your tea so we can head upstairs."

They'd taken to using Emalia's dressing room as a teaching

space. Cali found it the least distracting chamber in the small dwelling, and it offered the most area to move around in. Since moving into the apartment next door to Dasante, her expectation that her new living quarters would be a perfect place for magical training and practice had proved false. Tanyith still crashed on her couch but claimed he'd leave inside the week. *Which is good, because I'm not really the long-term houseguest type.*

Fyre snorted, and she looked at him. He currently circled much like a cat as a prelude to laying down in a safe corner. His ability to read her emotions seemed to have improved of late, almost to the point where he could understand her thoughts. She willed the idea of "bratty lizard" to him, but he didn't react.

Emalia stood at her wardrobe, her arms folded, and focused on where her student sat before her dressing table. "So, telepathy first."

Obediently, she locked away the distractions in her mind and reached inside for her magic. She sent out an intention to her great aunt to prime her to listen and be receptive to the message she was about to send. Then, she pushed her thoughts forward. *Your shoes are on fire.*

The woman glanced down but shook her head. "That is too much like a distraction. I didn't get the idea as a thought but as a feeling in my feet. You need to separate those two approaches."

She frowned as she thought the critique through. "Okay, let me try again." This time, she focused on the words themselves rather than the ideas behind them and pictured the letters in her brain.

Emalia grinned. "So much better, and yes, Invel is attractive and also, stop it."

Cali laughed. "Never."

"Try it with Fyre."

She twisted in her chair to face the Draksa and concentrated on sending him a message. He raised one lazy eyelid and winked at her, confirming he'd heard her request to do so. "Okay, I think I've got it. Will I be able to communicate over a long distance?"

Her teacher shrugged. "Maybe. That's up to you. You have the key now, so practice will make all the difference." Her tone conveyed pride at the achievement, then turned serious again. "Good. That is one thing accomplished. Let's move on to more direct mental influence."

"I discussed this with Dasante." She chuckled. "He said it sounds very much like cantrips from Dungeons and Dragons."

"I have no idea what that means. But do you think you should share everything with him?"

Cali nodded. "He knows all my other secrets. It's a little late to hide anything now."

"I'm sure you know best." Her tone suggested the opposite, but she had heard that caution often enough that it didn't really faze her anymore.

"I gotta trust someone or I'll wind up alone like some other people I know."

A small smile surfaced, only to be quickly banished with a scowl. "Impudent whelp. Let's get on with it. Prepare your mind as if you were about to cast a distraction but this time, instead of going the subtle way around your opponent's mental barrier, you'll use focused force to pierce it. When I do it, I imagine my will is a needle stabbing through a balloon with enough precision to not pop it."

The girl frowned. So much of mental magic had turned out to be building one's own metaphors and often, hers were not in alignment with her teacher's. Still, it was a place to start. She pictured Emalia's mind before her as a balloon, stretched her will, and focused it into a sharp point. When it reached the edge, the barrier's resistance held her at bay. She began to search for the spaces between as she'd done before, then stopped and forced herself to refocus.

With intense concentration, she pushed against the resistance and suddenly broke through the outer seal. Two more pushes took her inside. Again, she returned to old habits, tried to make Emalia's nose itch, and cursed inwardly. She imagined her great aunt's mind as a computer waiting for a program and told her brain to make her sneeze.

The loud noise snapped her out of her inward focus, and she grinned as Fyre jumped, startled by the sound. Her aunt raised an eyebrow as she dabbed her face with the handkerchief she always had hidden somewhere on her. "It's exactly like you to choose something so messy."

Cali grinned. "I thought if it was against your nature it would be harder."

Her teacher laughed. "Lies. You did it because you're a brat."

She stood and stretched. "Yeah, okay, you got me."

"Are you headed to the library next, then?"

"No, homework this afternoon and work tonight," she

replied and sighed. "I'll try to get there tomorrow after the dojo."

The older woman crossed the room and wrapped her in a hug. "You're over-committed. Maybe you should give something up now that you have extra money from your parents."

Cali squeezed her in return, then released her and stepped back with a smile. "I wouldn't know what to do with free time. Keeping busy keeps me from worrying, which is all good." She snapped her fingers, then growled impatiently. "Fyre, come on, lazybones." He struggled to his feet and she summoned a portal to her new apartment. When he sauntered through, she rolled her eyes at his attitude and gave Emalia a mischievous grin. "Say hi to Invel for me," she called as she stepped into the rift and closed it behind her to cut off any reply. *Heh. It's nice to have the last word for a change.*

CHAPTER THREE

Zeb wiped the bar carefully and made sure the polishing cloth touched every part of its surface. Unknown to anyone who lacked the requisite experience to identify it, the wood was not from Earth. He'd brought it over himself by direct portal into the Drunken Dragons tavern with the help of his only brother, who held a similar position at a similarly named inn on Oriceran. The unique piece of furniture connected them and grounded him in his new home without sacrificing his attachment to his former one.

He was sure some of the council members were sufficiently savvy to recognize it but also assumed they'd understand. Not that he particularly cared what others thought—with precious few exceptions—but he did have some significant pride wrapped up in the bar. In another decade or so, the timber would be suitably saturated with the oil he used and be ready for carving. He looked forward to spending his empty moments working on it. Although, if the business continued to be as steady as it had been that night, he might not live long enough to see it completed.

Cali made a circuit of the last lingering customers, all of whom should have been out the door ten minutes before when the tavern's official closing time came and went unnoticed. He shouted, "Okay, away with y'all. The girl has studying to do." She scowled at him for reminding her. *That'll teach her to complain where I can hear her.* He offered a wide grin in reply, and she shook her head and began to verbally and sometimes physically push their patrons toward the exit.

The dwarf locked the door behind her fifteen minutes later, which left barely enough time to get ready for the meeting. A quick series of words invoked the wards around the tavern, which he'd added to since the human and Atlantean gangs had become interested in it. He bustled downstairs and levitated several crates out of the way, then placed his hands on two small protrusions and muttered a command. The wall slid away to reveal a room beyond it, dominated by a large round table. Seven chairs and seven glasses were already positioned, as were the casks of red wine, white wine, and his own autumn mulled cider.

He opened the hole in the magical defenses protecting the building and a portal appeared immediately. Malonne the Light Elf, first to arrive as always, stepped through with a nod and headed to the refreshments. New portals materialized on schedule, one per minute, until the group was assembled.

Small talk accompanied the filling of glasses, but a diffuse sense of urgency inspired everyone to take their places quickly around the table. When he lowered himself into the final seat, the eldest of the council, Vizidus the wizard, spoke with what sounded like deep concern. "Thank you all for coming tonight and as always, thank you to Zeb for hosting us." They exchanged nods, and the old man pushed a stray hair from his white mane out of his face. "Events move in the direction we expected and may soon require a response from us. It would be prudent to share our perspectives now, rather than when time is an urgent factor." He gestured to his left and invited the next being to speak.

One of the things Zeb found interesting about his compatriots was their habit of choosing a different chair each time they gathered. It was not something he saw often in the tavern above, where most of his patrons had a favorite seat and didn't change unless forced to. He always made sure to be the last to sit at the council gatherings, which allowed him to observe their choices. Tonight, Scoppic was in the chair to Vizidus's left and looked decidedly bookish with his round glasses, neatly braided white beard and trimmed mustache, and soft face. His long wavy white hair and ornate burgundy waistcoat completed the look. The latter's gold buttons winked in the flickering light from the fireplace. The gnome coughed once before he spoke, his voice thin and high-pitched. "Our neighborhood has not been affected. Still, we see the gangs on the streets and in the shops and know it's only a matter of time until someone comes to us."

Zeb nodded, as did several others. The city's gnomes lived mainly near the library and museum in the most affluent section of the Garden District. The area wouldn't be on the front edge of the territorial expansion, but neither would it escape the determined forces that wrestled for control of the city. Beside Scoppic sat Delia, an aggressive witch who was rumored to be quite powerful. He'd never seen her in action, but the intensity in her eyes added weight to the stories that people he trusted had shared. She was clad in a Loyola sweatshirt and black jeans, and long sparkly earrings dangled within the rock-and-roll-messy black hair that tumbled over her shoulders and covered part of the school's logo.

The woman's voice was hoarse and sounded like every word had to be forced from her body. "Well, we are everywhere, and both the damn gangs are in our business on a daily basis. My people are seriously flipping tired of it. If we don't do something collectively, you can be damn sure me and mine will do something without you."

Vizidus shook his head gently, which made his own long hair—far stringier and whiter than hers—float about momentarily. "Surely it has not yet reached that point?"

The witch shrugged. "We have different opinions about what is tolerable, old friend. And my tolerance for their nonsense is rapidly reaching its end. With the power those at this table can bring to bear, we could eliminate both gangs easily."

Brukirot, the hulking Kilomea with the unexpectedly soft voice, nodded. "It's become clear that both the Zatoras and the Atlanteans will definitely not content themselves with taking territory solely from the human residents of the city. While my people are unlikely to be intimidated by any show of force that may emerge from either group, we must acknowledge that protecting all magicals from the humans' delusions of might and the Atlanteans' overreach is necessary. I suggest a concerted effort to take their soldiers off the streets in secrecy. In doing so, we could weaken both groups and frame the other for the action."

Zeb sighed. It was a good plan and reflected the Kilomean hunter instinct. Too often, humans and other magicals ascribed qualities to that race based on their size, which ranged from large to enormous. It failed to account for the nuanced skills that generations upon generations of experience hunting prey for food, sport, and pleasure had engendered in them. Brukirot was one of the smartest he'd come across. However, the giant's proposal was also overly optimistic and radiated confidence in the council's superiority that the dwarf didn't share.

Fortunately, he was next in line to speak. "I have two things to say. First, both gangs are aware of our interest in their activities. It is unlikely that we would manage to act in secret for long as their suspicions will naturally turn to us. Second, after the incident at the docks, it is to everyone's advantage to keep matters quiet. If we were to take a role, it would need to be more hidden and subtle than the plans that have been suggested so far. If we goad them into greater action, we risk damage to the innocent citizens of the city, which I'm sure we all agree must be avoided."

Lingering distrust of magicals was common more or less everywhere as the people of Earth came to terms with their changed reality. Even though there had been ample time to process the knowledge, the emotions inspired by an influx of aliens from another planet who possessed magical powers had proven harder for some to contend with.

Beside him, Malonne tapped his chin with elegant fingers and gemstones set in delicate rings glittered with the motion. His pale skin and light hair were a shade brighter than the off-white suit he wore. His words emerged slowly, which Zeb interpreted as thoughtful consideration.

"On one side of the scale lies the knowledge that we cannot stand idly by in the face of this threat. To do so would be entirely unacceptable. On the other, our involvement, if detected, risks increasing the danger to all." He lowered his hand to the table and drummed his manicured nails lightly to generate a decidedly annoying clicking sound. "So, if we are to act, we must do so with complete deniability as we cannot rely on secrecy." He nodded toward the dwarf, who returned the gesture. "I would contend that our best tools for the job are the ones already involved."

Invel, in the final seat, had remained inscrutable throughout the discussion. The Dark Elf's ashen hair and mottled skin made him look imperfect next to the Light Elf beside him. Intelligence radiated from him, and Zeb knew it was matched by cunning and a ruthless practicality when necessary. Unfortunately, the practical side was ascendant. "I agree. We should support those already in the gangs' sights—Caliste and Tanyith—as we have done since their first encounters with them."

Zeb winced. He'd hoped for something more substantial as an outcome. When he met Vizidus's eyes, he recognized the same sentiment in them. However, the others at the table nodded at the Drow's words, which meant the decision was essentially made.

Their leader asked, "Are all in agreement?" For the sake of unanimity, the dwarf signaled his assent along with the others. The wizard nodded. "So, on to other things," he said and the discussion turned to more common issues.

An hour later, everyone was gone except for Invel, who had raised his damaged leg and rested it on the chair the Light Elf had occupied. Their glasses had been refilled with the mulled cider, and he took an appreciative gulp. "Ah, Zeb, you are truly a master at the alcoholic arts."

He laughed. "What can I say? Sometimes, the stereotypes are true. Dwarves do enjoy a hearty drink from time to time."

"Like on the strike of every hour, day or night." The elf's grin was tired but no less mirthful for it.

"Nah, we have to sleep sometime. There are four or five hours without in there somewhere. But this is as potent as fruit juice for me as far as intoxication goes."

"Ah, to have been born among your people would have been a wonderful thing."

"We all have our advantages, my friend. Speaking of which, what do you know that I should know?"

Invel held his cup out, and Zeb carried it to the cask. The Drow drank half of the new serving, then set it on the table. "The great aunt asked me about the sword, among other things. There's no doubt, now, that it is in play."

Zeb shook his head. "How does an ancient Atlantean artifact end up here?"

His companion shrugged. "New Orleans has been peopled by magicals more or less since its founding. If a magical weapon was going to wind up anywhere, this certainly makes an eminently logical location."

"Do you know which one it is?"

"No. The pictures she shared weren't enough to tell. If I could put my hands on the other piece Caliste saw, I might be able to get somewhere."

The dwarf sighed. "I'm sure that's locked up safely somewhere, protected by wards and guards and who knows what other defenses." He assumed the Atlanteans would now rely on more than simply secrecy to ensure the safety of their prize.

The elf nodded. "Probably."

"Anything else?"

Invel grinned. "Nothing pertinent. I have some new things in the shop that might interest you—old weapons from Oriceran and interesting metals."

He waved a hand to push the idea away. "My forging days are behind me. Valerie was my last work. Now, I'm merely a simple innkeeper."

"So you say. But I noticed the way you straightened when Brukirot talked about removing some of the street soldiers. Your mind might be past the old days, but your heart isn't."

Zeb scowled. "My heart is exactly where it needs to be. Here, watching over all of you." He took the empty cup and filled it again, then handed it over. "This is your last glass. I won't carry you home again. I've had my fill of those particular strange looks."

The Drow laughed. "Are you afraid of being seen with a wicked Dark Elf?" It was a standing joke between them.

He snorted in false disgust. "Certainly not. But escorting a drunk one who's not all that good at walking when he's sober does nothing for my reputation as a tavern-keeper."

Invel put a hand over his heart. "You wound me. And yes, I'm wounded. Deeply. Tragically. Wounded."

The dwarf rolled his eyes. "I'm fairly sure that's your exit cue."

"No, I'm sure I have a better one. Wait, let me think for a second."

"Trust me, that was your closing line. It's time to depart. Leave the audience wanting more. Go, you buffoon."

Laughing, his guest pushed to his feet and walked mostly steadily to the unwarded portion of the room. Moments later, his portal vanished behind him. Zeb chuckled quietly as he cleaned and mused on the fact that while the Drow might seem to be less influential than the others at the table, he was the first one he would want at his back in the face of real trouble. *And if things keep going the way they are, we could see that face before too long.*

CHAPTER FOUR

Zeb's urgency to push her out the door the night before had been the catalyst for uneasy dreams. While Cali had always been dimly aware of the presence of a council of magicals present in the city, she never imagined that she would somehow be noticed by it, much less become an unofficial influence upon it via her boss's membership.

So, when her phone rang with the sounds of "Rock Me Amadeus"—she resisted the urge to pound on the wall and wake Dasante up for adding that particular song to her playlist—she was more than willing to get out of bed and start her day. She ran her bare foot over the scales on Fyre's back and, as always, marveled at the way they managed to be strong enough to protect him but still completely soft to the touch.

In addition to the joy of not having to share a bathroom with the other members of the boardinghouse, her new apartment also boasted a seemingly unlimited supply of hot water. She luxuriated under it for as long as she could but marked the passing minutes off in her mind until she had to dry herself, get dressed, and head to the dojo.

She left the apartment quietly so as to not wake Tanyith, who slept on the couch. Allegedly, he would move out today, although there'd been some small possibility of a delay. He wasn't a bad roommate and they mostly stayed out of each other's way, but she was ready to have the space to herself. Well, Fyre would be there, of course, but they were a team now. Where the one went, the other would go, and that basically meant always.

Except for that morning, apparently. When she'd tried to rouse the Draksa, he'd merely rolled onto his back and studiously ignored her. With a muttered, "Traitor," she had popped her earphones in and put on her jogging playlist for the run to Sensei Ikehara's dojo.

It was a typical start to a New Orleans day outside, the temperature already climbing. The streets were quiet except for dedicated revelers still up from the night before and the city's early shift on the way to work. As her feet pounded the pavement and the music swirled in her head, she drew on her magic and sent it out in a broad circle around her in a query for danger. So far, the practice had not produced any results, but she was hopeful that it might give her at least a little warning if an attack should materialize unexpectedly.

Frankly, waiting for the Atlanteans to make their move had become a stress of its own. They had promised seven days, and that deadline had passed almost a week before. Since then, she'd kept a watchful eye on her surroundings in search of trouble. The delay in its appearance suggested she wasn't their first priority or that the adventure at the docks had changed the timetable or something. All she knew for sure was that the fight would happen eventually, and she would do her best to be ready for it the instant it did.

Thus, when she arrived at the rear entrance to the dojo and discovered an envelope with her name on it stuck to the door, it wasn't as big a shock as it might otherwise have been. The flowing letters were beautiful, almost calligraphic, and looked to have been written with a pen so fancy it would probably take her a month's pay to afford one. She detached it and carefully cracked the ornate wax stamp with an unknown seal that held the heavy envelope closed.

The message inside was simple and to the point.

Caliste Leblanc. The time for your reckoning is at hand. Appear at the location on the map within at four o'clock. Failure to do so will result in the destruction of the dojo where you train, the tavern where you work, and the boardinghouse in which you live, in addition to your own execution.

Well, at least they haven't caught on to my change of address. That's not necessarily good, though, since it puts Mrs. Jackson and her tenants in unnecessary danger. The note was unsigned. A piece of paper with a hand-drawn map on it was enclosed, directing her to what was labeled as a school.

She sighed. *Awesome, way too much time to dwell on my fate. There's no reason not to clean and practice this morning.* She chuckled grimly. *Who knows? Whatever I learn might come in handy later today.*

When the class was over, Cali portaled to the apartment and discovered that Tanyith had indeed removed his belongings from the living room and was gone. "It's probably for the best," she announced to the empty space. "He would insist on coming along, and that wouldn't work at all." She headed into the bedroom to find that Fyre had moved from his place on the floor to the bed and blinked sleepy eyes at her. She flopped onto the mattress, her head next to his. "Guess what, long, dark, and scaly. We have a date for a fight later."

The Draksa pushed himself into a seated position and stretched his neck toward the ceiling. "Who have you offended now?"

She shrugged. "Based on the language and the elegance of the note, my guess is that it's the Atlanteans." She tossed the paper beside him. He looked at it for a moment and snorted.

"It's about time."

Cali laughed. "Right?" She stood with a groan and paced slowly through the room. "So from what I've been told, each of the ritual battles increases the numbers on each side as a measure of how many allies one can convince to help them out or something. This fight will be two on two. You, of course, are my first choice of partner."

He snorted again. "Naturally. As if any other solution would be acceptable."

She nodded. "And unfortunately, the only weapons allowed are magical ones, so I can't simply bring in an Uzi and spray the place with lead or anything."

"You'd be more likely to hurt yourself with a gun than damage anyone else, based on what I've seen of your dexterity." His tone was teasing, and she rewarded him with an extended tongue and single finger.

"So, I have my sticks, you have your skills, and we have all the strategies we've worked on together. I would think that should be enough to overcome whatever they might throw at us."

His snout dipped and rose in a nod. "Still, a backup plan is never a bad thing."

A quick nod indicated agreement. "I thought about that while I got the dojo ready this morning. Now that Dasante knows the truth about you and me, we can impose on him for that. In fact, let's have a chat with him about it."

He answered the door readily at her knock and ushered the two of them into his apartment. It was a mirror to hers in layout but was better furnished. He'd explained that whenever other people moved out and left furniture, he took the nicer pieces and traded them for his own less appealing versions. His laugh had sounded slightly embarrassed as he confided, "Sometimes, it's good to be the person in charge." His role as the caretaker for the building on behalf of his mother and stepfather made him uncomfortable, that much was clear, but she liked that he seemed to take advantage of the perks it afforded him.

She extended a flip phone to him. He took it, turned it over in his hands, and chuckled. "The ultimate in decades-old technology. Gee, thanks, Cal." She punched him in the arm, and he gave a small yelp that inspired a smile.

"Don't be a chucklehead if you can help it, okay?" She pointed at the device. "It's got two numbers in it. Mine and Detective Barton's. If I'm not back here tonight by, say, seven o'clock, send her to this address." She handed him the map she'd received, which was already locked in her memory.

Her friend looked at her like she had said the words in a foreign language. "Of course I'll do it, but why?"

Cali shrugged. "I have a date with some Atlanteans and I'm not sure how it will turn out. You're my backup plan."

A hint of alarm entered his voice. "Are you going alone?"

She shook her head. "Okay, it's probably better to say you're my backup backup plan. Fyre will come with me."

His relief was palpable. He nodded. "This is the one you've waited for, then, right?"

"It seems like it is."

"And there's no way out of it?"

"Maybe," she responded uncertainly, "but I would have to believe they won't make good on their threats to hurt innocent people who have the misfortune of knowing me. Unfortunately, I don't think they're bluffing."

He looked down, tapped the phone with his index finger, and was silent for a couple of seconds, then met her gaze. "How about having the police ready for them when they arrive? Roll the whole gang up at once?"

"If only." She sighed. "They won't bring everyone, and even though there might be some important people there, they'd probably be able to delay the police at least long enough to escape. That's the best-case scenario. The worst-case is too many dead men and women in blue uniforms. No, I think we need to do as they say. Fortunately, they seem constrained by their weird rules regarding Atlantean ritual combat. I plan to research it when I go to the library."

He laughed. "So you finally gave in?"

She frowned at him. "I did not give in. I was never against the idea but I have so much going on. Perhaps you've noticed."

His grin preceded a nod of acknowledgment. "Well, at the very least, you should wear that awesome jacket from the Drow. Extra padding could come in handy. And, hey, try not to be killed, okay? I don't want to have to look for a new tenant this soon after finding one."

"I'll do my best," she said with a dramatic eye-roll. "See you tonight."

Cali used her phone to guide her to the location, which was across the city and in a residential area. It was clearly abandoned—probably a high school based on its size—and the side door had been knocked from its hinges. She climbed over it and moved deeper into the structure. A faint glowing trail shimmered on the tiles, and she followed it with Fyre close beside her. He was in his usual disguise as a Rottweiler in case they came upon something unexpected. She'd listened to Dasante's advice and wore the tough leather jacket zipped over her t-shirt. Black jeans and boots finished the outfit. Her fingers moved rhythmically to circle her wrists as she walked, comforted by the feel of the heavy magical bracelets.

The luminescent path ended at the gymnasium where she found exactly nothing unexpected. A crowd of onlookers were present like the time before and surrounded a rectangular basketball court that would doubtless be the combat arena. The same man she'd fought previously stood with his arms folded at the opposite side from the doorway. His muscles were still large, although they were hidden under a baggy sweatshirt of some kind instead of on display under the tight shirt he'd worn before. His dark skin and tightly braided hair shone under the weird lighting, and his long beard had been clipped to a short goatee. Tactical pants and boots finished his look.

Beside him stood the witch who'd overseen the last bout, presumably to act as his partner. She'd traded her simple dress for a tight tunic and camouflage pants with sand-colored army boots. The necklace with arcane symbols still hung around her neck. The long hair she hadn't paid attention to before was bound in a long braid that rested on her shoulder. Cali scanned the crowd quickly and her gaze stopped at the sight of a familiar woman in an expensive suit.

Danna stepped forward and directed a grin at her. "Cali, it's so good to see you again."

She scowled. "Are you gonna lock me in a box again, wench?"

Her laugh was condescending. "Well, if there's enough left of you at the end of the battle to put in one, rest assured I will. And I'll return it to the tavern so your friends can remember your failure after we take the business over."

Now, it was her turn to laugh. "Please. I've already proven to be more than a match for muscles over there, and my second will make mincemeat out of his partner. He'll chew her leg off before she knows what hit her."

The Atlantean leader shook her head. "We underestimated you once—twice if you want to include our first meeting. It won't happen a third time. And no one here is fooled by the nature of your partner."

Cali waved and Fyre dropped the illusion. Several indrawn breaths greeted the sight of the dragon lizard. His metallic scales shimmered in rainbow colors under the industrial lights from high above. "My statement stands. Bargain bin Jason Momoa and the Wicked Witch of the West over there won't be a match for us."

Danna shrugged. "Then you'll be one step closer to your victory, not that you'll ever reach it."

She sighed. "Do we really need to do this? Couldn't you all simply, you know, head back to New Atlantis and leave my city alone?"

This time, the woman's laugh was throaty and almost seductive. "Oh, no, princess. Soon, the city will be entirely ours, and you will come begging to have a place in it."

"Over my dead body."

The evil grin widened. "That's the plan." She stepped back and cleared the path for the fight to begin.

Cali looked at Fyre with a grin of her own. "Which one do you want?" He jerked his head toward the right to indicate the witch, and she nodded. "Good. As long as you keep her busy, it shouldn't take me too long to disable the meathead. After that, we can finish her together and be done in more than enough time for me to get to work."

She turned to her two opponents, raised one hand, and crooked a finger at the man. "Bring it, big boy."

He attacked instantly, an eagerness to start the battle that equaled her own visible in his gritted teeth and wild eyes.

CHAPTER FIVE

F yre was a blur in her peripheral vision as he raced toward the witch. Cali set her feet to withstand her opponent's assault. She reminded herself that escalations would bring retaliatory escalations and to focus on keeping it hand-to-hand for as long as possible. Avoiding the trident that had so vexed her the time before seemed like a very good plan.

His charge ended with a sudden leap and his foot snapped out at her chest. She flinched instinctively, then continued the motion and fell away from the kick so it barely grazed her shoulder. He was out of range before she had a chance to counterattack, and she lunged toward him. When he landed and lashed out with a back kick, it was a move she'd anticipated. She grasped his leg with both hands, fell back to the floor, and twisted it over her head. He had no option except to spin horizontally if he wanted to avoid having his knee dislocated, and he landed hard on his back. His other foot drove down from above, and she rolled to escape it and scrambled in the hope that she could gain her feet before he recovered.

She succeeded, and as he straightened, she delivered a sidekick to his ribs. The blow struck padding of some kind under his loose athletic jacket, and he flicked a grin at her. *Well, apparently, he's smart enough to learn something. Good for him and bad for me.* He brought an elbow down on her shin, and she cursed as she staggered away.

The Atlantean pressed his advantage and lurched at her while she struggled to find her balance on the injured leg. She evaded his jab with a quick sidestep, ducked under his hook punch, and almost bent herself in half backward to evade the uppercut that carried his full power behind it. Instinctively, she turned the backbend into a hands-assisted flip—one of the few acrobatic moves she was capable of—and came up ready to defend herself.

He snarled and shuffled in, then drove his rear arm forward with a twist of his hips to aim his fist at her forehead. She swayed to the side, caught his wrist, and punched her knuckles into the nerve cluster above his elbow. With his arm weakened from the strike, she used it to yank him off balance and push him toward the floor. He twisted his body violently and wrenched his limb out of her grasp.

Her adversary stood opposite her, shook the damaged limb, and growled with suppressed fury. "Okay, little girl. That's one for you. But now, it's my turn."

Fyre's plan had been to overwhelm the witch with a

sudden rush and relied on the likelihood that she would underestimate exactly how fast he could be and expect him to take to the air. Even though the room's ceiling was two stories high, it would nonetheless hamper his ability to attack from above as he couldn't get up far enough for a proper dive. His swift advance involved shifting from side to side, the serpentine motion a natural and effective instinct for his species.

It proved valuable yet again when the blasts of shadow magic the witch flung at him passed on all sides but failed to connect. With only a moment before he would reach her, she abandoned the attacks and threw up a shadow barrier between them. The Draksa darted to the right and conjured a veil that curved almost all the way to the line of onlookers in an attempt to sneak behind her protective wall.

The witch snarled and waved her hand in a wide arc to deliver glitter in a sparkling rain through the surrounding space. It was drawn to him despite the veil—a type of magic he hadn't seen before and didn't know how to counter—and he dispelled the illusion. She scythed a narrow line of shadow at his feet, and he elevated hastily as it sliced a clean groove into the gymnasium floor. Her other hand whipped toward him and another line of shadow emanated from it, as thin as a beam of light but undeniably wickedly sharp and destructive. He banked to the side to avoid it and found his progress instantly hindered by the back wall of the room. With a snarl, he pulled up and rotated so his feet pointed down and his teeth faced his foe and without pause, dove directly at her.

One of the shadow lances cut across his wing and he

howled in pain and anger as it parted the scales and the flesh beneath. His claws stretched toward the witch, and a tearing sound confirmed that he'd snagged the shoulder of her tunic as she dropped and rolled away. Fyre landed in a scramble of claws, slid on the slick surface, and managed to reorient himself quickly. He expelled a cone of frost at her, but she summoned a shadow shield to protect herself and the frozen particles flowed around her without effect.

Frustration roiled his mind, but the joy of combat surged in his heart. With a deep, throaty growl, he launched himself at her again.

Her foe's long dark braids whipped around him as he attacked. He had abandoned the previously ineffective boxing style and was now a constant blur of motion. His approach was graceful and unpredictable as it involved steps, skips, and small jumps that made any interruption to his advance too difficult to manage. Cali remained loose, kept her balance evenly distributed, and waited for the actual attack. When it came, it was a surprise, nonetheless.

He raised his arms and telegraphed a punch, and as her body reacted to it instinctively, he hurled himself into a lightning flip that whipped his feet at her in a blur. With an undignified yelp, she skittered to the side and barely managed to avoid taking a heel to the head. The strike of his heavy boot on her shoulder sent a red haze across her senses and she staggered away. He dove forward, planted one hand on the ground, and used it as a pivot to swing his boots at her face. She thrust them away frantically and this time, the only damage was a stinging blow to the forearm she used to block, which went numb from the impact. As soon as his feet found purchase, he launched up again and aimed a jumping sidekick at her chest. She raised her arms in defense but the strike pounded into them and she careened away.

With a muttered oath, she fell and slid on the slippery floor, thankful for the padding in the jacket Nylotte had given her, which had probably saved her from broken bones. Before her momentum stopped, she used it to roll into a backward somersault and rise to her feet. He had already surged into another assault, but the shock and anger at being hit had accelerated her brain. When he repeated the flip, she rotated sideways with a quick stutter-step and pistoned a kick into the side of his knee as soon as his foot landed. The Atlantean crumpled but pushed off with his other leg to gain enough distance that her follow-up attack fell short. He rolled to his feet with a grin. "Piti-ful. Is that all you have?" He flicked his braids out of his face.

Cali shook her head. "I beat you once and I'll beat you again." Her palms itched for the feel of her sticks but she still believed facing his trident would be more dangerous than dealing with his hand-to-hand combat skills. She offered him a condescending grin. "I'll admit your dancing was something of a surprise, but that's the thing with surprises—once they're revealed, they're easily dealt with."

Her provocation failed to elicit the desired reaction. The enforcer merely smiled and advanced again.

Fyre was ready for the shadow lance as it streaked out to strike at his feet again. This time, instead of launching fully into the air, he made a small hop assisted by a wave of his wings and veered to the side. It didn't appear to be an attack the witch could sustain for long, as her routine was to summon the line, slash with it, and let it dissipate. If the weapon had been more permanent, his evasion wouldn't have worked. He sent another blast of frost at her as a distraction and surged forward at an angle. She cowered behind the protection of her shield to avoid the icy blast as he'd hoped she would. He spun as he arrived in range and whipped his tail behind her.

The heavily muscled appendage smacked into her calves and she immediately fell. Her skull made a resounding crack when it met the wooden surface, followed by a series of loud curses as she regained her feet. The scent of her blood wafted to him and drew a fierce smile. She'd landed the first strike, but he was fairly sure he'd done far more damage with his retaliatory blow. As she swung her hands to bring her shadow magic to bear, he caught sight of the very small wands held in each and hopped to the side as another line of shadow emanated from one of them. His jump was intercepted by a sudden wave of her other hand, which conjured a wall of force that pounded into him and propelled him in the direction in which he was already moving. He landed and skidded on his flank to scatter the onlookers in his path before his spine impacted with the bleachers.

The Draksa twisted into an upright position with a growl. It had been a clever attack and one he hadn't expected, but she didn't follow it up in the seconds during which he was vulnerable. Instead, she swayed for a moment with her eyelids closed, then opened them again with a smile. The only conclusion he could draw from the focused awareness in her gaze was that she had used her magic to block the pain or to heal herself. Not that his kind gambled, generally speaking.

He checked on his partner and saw that she was injured but still fighting. Rage surged through him at the sight but he forced it back and moved cautiously toward his opponent. He and Cali had discussed strategy ahead of time and had concurred that the rules of the battle probably ensured that as long as they stayed with their selected target, their foes would be required to do the same. So, while he wanted to rescue her, he couldn't. They'd agreed they would only cross opponents if their enemies did it first or if the need was so great that it left no other option.

Fyre belched another barrage of ice at the witch and again, she summoned a shadow shield to protect herself. He maintained the assault as he advanced, which forced her to stay cowered and covered, and tensed his muscles for a second tail strike.

Her opponent used a mix of his direct and indirect styles as he renewed his advance. When he tried the flip kick again, she was ready for it and skittered out of range. As soon as he had regained his balance, he launched a punch at her temple that would have knocked her into the next century if it had connected.

Cali flinched to allow the strike to pass in front of her

and used her left fist to guide his arm away. She caught his wrist with her right hand and yanked him forward, then controlled the joint with a sharp twist as she ducked under the limb, spun so her back faced him, and hammered an elbow into his ribs. He grunted at the impact, but she didn't feel anything break and cursed under her breath. *Whatever he's wearing seems to have as much protection as the jacket Nylotte gave me. I hate competent enemies.*

She raised her other hand to his trapped wrist and pulled down sharply in an attempt to snap his elbow over her shoulder. His response was unexpected, and she felt rather than saw him flip over her head. When he landed, he planted a sidekick into her chest, which drove her back a step and stole her breath. She managed to not fall and pushed forward to counter when he moved faster than he had in either battle. This time, his flip came in at an angle instead of from the top, and her frantic effort to shuffle out of danger failed. His feet struck her left shoulder and forearm. The cracking sound promised a fracture or break lower in the limb, and the way her arm suddenly screamed fire at her and hung limply told the tale of a dislocated shoulder, based on her many viewings of *Lethal Weapon*.

The Atlantean enforcer stepped back and laughed, which helped her to master her pain and transform it into a simmering cold rage. She shouted, "Fyre, now," and willed the bracelet on her right hand to become an Escrima stick. The sight of the Draksa bathing the enforcer in ice made her smile, but it quickly turned to a frown as a shadow shield stopped the freeze at his thighs and the blasted trident appeared in his hand. *Okay, jerk. So you want to take it up a notch? Let's get to it.*

CHAPTER SIX

The Atlantean enforcer used his magical trident to break away the ice that had gathered around his feet, then threw the weapon at the Draksa. Fyre leapt to avoid it and flapped his wings to gain height. Cali noticed that he seemed to favor one of them. She made a wish that he wasn't too badly injured and pushed down the additional rage that his injury inspired. *I have plenty, thanks.* Fortunately, the quick healing powers of his species gave him a greater ability to sustain damage than she possessed.

She raced forward with the held stick in her right hand and winced at each uncontrolled swing of her dislocated left arm. With a cry of surprise, she threw herself to the side to avoid another throw of the forked weapon, which had magically returned to the man's fist. Fortunately, she had reflexively dodged to the right and landing on that shoulder was nothing more than an inconvenience. She scrambled to her feet as her enemy kicked away the remaining ice that had trapped him.

Entirely focused on regaining her balance, she didn't

notice the powerful blast of water until it swept into the side of her head and flung her violently to sprawl on her back. She rolled sideways and searched for the source. The witch directed another focused line of liquid at Fyre and thrust him off course. The dragon lizard landed quickly to avoid any further attacks while airborne.

His wing must be bothering him more than I thought. Normally, the Draksa was more agile in the air than on the ground, which was saying something given his earth-bound prowess. She yelled, "Back on the witch," and once again scrabbled to her feet as her partner crossed in front of her and returned his focus to their female opponent.

She focused her attention on the enforcer, who strode forward with the trident in his hands. He flipped it to horizontal and fired a force blast from its tines, but she side-stepped it easily. "Been there, done that, got the t-shirt," she taunted. He tried again and this time, slashed it viciously to generate a sustained line of force along that vector. She simply spun to the side to avoid it and continued to close the distance between them.

The stick in her hand hampered her ability to launch direct magical assaults, and her dangling arm was equally useless for that task. She saw her opportunity when he abandoned the magic in favor of a direct attack—maybe he wanted to make it personal. *That suits me fine, buddy.*

He stabbed with the trident and aimed at her heart. Cali circled her stick from outside to in and up to down to deflect the attack to her right as she sidestepped so it couldn't catch her if the block missed. She flicked her weapon hard at his face and caught him a glancing blow on the cheek as he jerked away, which accomplished nothing more than to increase his anger. He spun the forked weapon hand over hand in front of him. The action turned it into a blur before he lunged it suddenly at her face. She shifted her head left, then right, then ducked to avoid the third attack. When she threw the stick forehand at his knee, it connected with a pleasing crack.

With her hand temporarily free, she punched the air with a fist and a force blow hammered into the same knee and forced it out from under him. He caught himself on the way down but the distraction opened him to her punch at his face, and his nose broke under the impact of her force magic. He snarled and hurled the trident at her. The angle was bad but it still compelled her to drop and roll away. She'd momentarily forgotten about the damage to her arm, but the devastating wave of pain that seared through her when it impacted with the floor was an immediate and effective reminder. A curse fought free between her gritted teeth as she staggered to her feet and called her stick to her. Her foe mirrored her and his weapon slapped into his hand. He shook his head and it seemed like he no longer enjoyed the battle nearly as much as he had at the beginning. "It's time to end this."

She nodded. "So, you surrender?" His snarl suggested that wasn't his intent at all.

Fyre decided he'd had enough of the enemy witch. The blast of water had been more annoying than painful, but the damage the shadow lance had done to his wing was healing more slowly than he would've expected, probably because he put it constantly under strain in the battle. She fired a staccato line of shadow bolts at him, and he dodged them with ease as his serpentine advance again caused them to miss. He rushed in and swiped with his tail, but she managed a shadow shield to block it. While her attention was focused on his tail, he raked his talons at her legs and rent the camouflage pants she wore. She screamed as blood flowed, and he growled a laugh at her.

He was too close to avoid the force blast she fired with both hands, and it hurled him violently away while he twisted to slow his momentum. From nearby, Cali called, "Switch," and as he landed, he spun and charged the man she'd been fighting. The attack clearly surprised the enforcer, and Fyre's claws scored the boots at the backs of his calves as he flashed past. The Draksa changed direction, anticipating a counterattack, and took a glancing blow from a blast of energy released by the trident.

He whirled with a growl and snaked in toward the man, who spun his weapon several times before he thrust it out in a stabbing motion. The dragon lizard was faster, and he dodged easily while he continued to close the distance. He stopped suddenly and breathed heartily, and a cone of frost surged toward his adversary. The Atlantean spun the trident again, and it redirected the icy blast upward before he countered with another force bolt. Fyre vaulted up to avoid it, flapped his wings once, and extended his claws toward the man's face.

The pain in her arm had turned to numbness and her brain

mercifully shut off the warning system once it discovered that she didn't pay attention. She rocketed into an attack on the witch and counted on the change of opponents to give her an edge. When the woman raised her arms, she hurled her stick at her enemy's face. The surprise move made the witch flinch, and although she batted the projectile away, it was enough distraction for Cali to get close. She delivered a front kick to the woman's stomach that doubled her over, then a snap kick to the side of her leg that brought her down to one knee.

Before she could deliver a decisive blow, her adversary managed to raise one hand and fire a shadow beam that burned into her leg. The damaged limb buckled, and she turned it into a forward tackle. Her opponent landed a weak elbow to her head while she maneuvered into position, then squealed in pain when Cali's legs clamped around hers and her right arm slithered around her throat. Her feet pressed the woman's knee in one direction and her shin in the other, locked the joint, and caused her to flail madly from the pain. *I only have to hold it long enough until she passes out.* Chokeholds were always the last resort for her because the danger of accidentally killing the other person involved was significant. Still, if there was ever anyone she'd want to do serious damage to, the sneering witch ranked high on the list.

Her foe keened again as she readjusted her legs. When the woman wrenched against the hold, the leg lock slipped. Although her lower leg broke with a loud snap, the desperate move allowed her to wriggle free of the chokehold. She blasted her adversary's face with shadow and thrust her head against the floor hard enough to fill her vision with stars. Cali summoned her stick to her hand and lashed out before the attack could be repeated, and the woman rolled off her. She sensed the witch gathering power for a final blow and whispered, "*Aspida*," to activate her shield charm.

Quickly, she segmented a piece of her mind and focused on finding her partner. His uniqueness among the creatures in the room made him easy to identify, and she pushed a thought into his brain. The wash of approval that returned to her signaled his acceptance of her request. Moments after the witch detonated a force blast that battered her shield and knocked her back several feet, the Draksa coated the woman in ice. Meanwhile, from her position mostly hidden by the dragon lizard and the enemy witch, she let her shield fall, summoned all her magical strength, and thrust it in a punch at the Atlantean enforcer. It caught him directly in the forehead and he staggered and fought to keep his balance. She tried to rise, but her leg buckled again. Instead, she threw her stick at him, and while his groggy brain focused on the incoming projectile, she delivered another force punch. He fell, unconscious before he landed.

Fyre stepped beside her and used his snout to help her into a seated position, then eventually, to stand using him as support. Danna stepped forward from the crowd, her slow clap the only sound in the room. Grudging respect was present in her tone. "I didn't believe you would survive this round. Congratulations. The next battle will be three on three, and you have two weeks to prepare for it. During that time, as long as you do not attack any of us, none of us will attack you." She pointed at several of her underlings, and one of them opened a portal while two others went to assist the defeated Atlantean champions.

Cali growled, "When does this end?"

The woman in the suit laughed. "Why, when you lose, of course."

"That won't happen. I won't lose to any of you."

"It is inevitable. There are many of us and not that many of you. Eventually, you'll run out of allies, but I never will."

It took several minutes for the Atlanteans to vanish. Cali and Fyre kept their guards up the whole time, fearful of a surprise attack despite the woman's words. In the end, though, it didn't materialize, and she collapsed with a loud moan. She swallowed the healing potion she'd brought and was surprised that even after the rush of warmth flowed through her, neither her arm nor leg felt fully healed. With her good hand, she dug her phone out and called Dasante. When he asked if she was okay, she laughed. "Not quite. Call Zeb, tell him where I am, and ask him to bring another healing potion." She dropped the cell and turned toward Fyre. "I'll take a little nap. Wake me up when..." Her voice trailed off as darkness filled her vision and she fell into unconsciousness.

CHAPTER SEVEN

Tanyith rose from his chair when the Drow arrived and extended a hand. "Thank you so much for meeting me."

Nylotte nodded and took the seat across the table as he reclaimed his own. He'd chosen one of the city's better under-the-radar seafood restaurants for their meeting. The exterior was dilapidated and the hand-painted *Stephan's* sign weathered and in need of renewal. Inside, though, the eatery was cool and crisp, both in temperature and in design. The square tables that filled the dining floor were a little closer together than he would've preferred, but their starched white tablecloths and bright red elegantly folded cloth napkins communicated a subtle elegance that made a customer feel as if they'd wandered into a retreat from the outside world.

And, after more failures than successes in tracking down Sienna's ex-boyfriend, a break from those pressures was very welcome. The Dark Elf across from him looked like a performer or a rock-and-roll star with her long white hair unconfined and wild and a form-fitting scarlet tunic with far too many silver buttons over black leather pants. Her expression, as it had been most of the times he'd been in her presence, gave away nothing useful other than a vague sense of irritation atop the fundamental intensity that radiated from the woman.

She flicked her napkin open and deposited it in her lap in an elegant movement, then put her elbows on the table and laced her fingers. Nylotte looked over them and met his gaze. "So, Tanyith, what's so urgent that I needed to come to this sweltering city of yours?"

He laughed. "As if you don't have enough magic to be at whatever temperature you like."

Her wave was casually dismissive. "Magic is for important things, not petty comforts."

His reply was forestalled by the arrival of their server, a tall man in a white dress shirt and black trousers. His Atlantean heritage was visible in his thick braids that every so often seemed to twitch with a life of their own. He took their orders and departed quickly, seeming unmoved by the presence of a Dark Elf in the restaurant. Even in New Orleans, which was home to a wide variety of magical species, Drow sightings were comparatively rare. She stared at him, and he sighed.

"My continued efforts to set up my own information sources have not met with grand success. Too much has changed since I was sent to Trevilsom prison. Not only the people I knew but the…" He paused to search for the right word. After a moment, he continued, "The currents, I guess, are unfamiliar and difficult to chart."

She nodded. "It was similar for me when I first went to

Stonesreach." Before meeting her, he hadn't been aware of the presence of a kemana beneath the city of Pittsburgh. The discovery had made him wonder whether one of the magical underground cities could be present in New Orleans, but with the high water table, he deemed it unlikely. *Although Atlantis and New Atlantis were built underwater, so who knows?*

"How did you overcome it?"

The woman shrugged. "Time, really. Plus, I established contacts among a wide variety of people with different circles of friends. Then, I found a way to make myself invaluable to all sides." She referred to her role as seller and trader of things magical, which had given her access to any number of individuals she otherwise might not have met. Ultimately, that was part of the reason she had been more or less compelled to help break him out, so he was grateful for whatever brought her to that point.

"That's good advice, although with the conflicting sides that have emerged here, it's a little difficult to bridge the gap. Speaking of which," he said and winced at the clumsy transition, "have you learned anything more about what went on at the docks? No one here has been able to shed any additional light on it."

Her reply was interrupted by the arrival of their lunch. They had elected to share a seafood boil, and the waiter cut a large net filled with crawfish, shrimp, lobster, corn, and potatoes and discharged the contents onto a silver platter he had placed between them. He provided each with a set of tongs to retrieve their food, freshened the ice waters both had selected, then departed quickly and professionally. They loaded their individual plates and tasted their first mouthfuls, and the smile on her face indicated that he had chosen the right restaurant.

Nylotte swallowed and took a sip of her water before she spoke. "Diana and her team have looked into it since then. They traced the ship's movements and it did make a scheduled stop at Jamaica, so it appears the story the people you rescued told you was true. There is a channel leading from New Atlantis to the islands and from there to here. Neither the agents nor I have any connections in the Caribbean, though, so we haven't been able to generate any more progress on that front."

He nodded. "Still, it's good to know the information we have is correct."

She speared a small potato and popped it in her mouth, then made an unexpectedly funny pleasure-face. He suppressed a laugh while he waited. She licked her lips. "Their computer tech managed to access satellite footage that gave partial recordings of the cruise ship while it was at sea. He caught a smaller vessel docking with it in the middle of nowhere. It positioned itself near one of the cargo doors, apparently. They've concluded that things were transferred between them, but the coverage was too sporadic and the image quality too poor to make out anything more definitive than that."

Tanyith drummed his fingers on the table. "So, not only do they bring people here illicitly, they bring stuff, too."

The Drow pointed her fork at him. "Very elegantly said." Her sarcasm was dry as the desert.

"I know, right?" He laughed. Something about her always made him feel off-center. "Is there anything else?"

"Actually, yes. They looked into the local police force

and found that your detective Kendra Barton is a good one. She has a clean record, considerable interaction with other agencies, and doesn't seem particularly interested in anything other than getting the job done and moving onto whatever is next. The rest of the organization is basically what you'd expect. There are some great officers and some less great officers but overall, it's positive. Which is impressive given how hard policing must be in a city like this."

He lowered his head in acknowledgment. While he had been part of the criminal element in the past, his gang had merely done what they needed to do to help recent arrivals to the city from New Atlantis. Technically, they skirted the edges of the law and hadn't become entangled with anything truly nefarious. *Speaking of which.* "Have you heard any whispers about drugs?"

She nodded, and the corners of her mouth turned down. "Unfortunately, yes. The human gang is involved in distributing all the usual drugs to both magicals and non-magicals. The Atlantean group, though, has really upped their game. They have something specifically for magicals that's already out on the street. It's highly addictive from what my sources say, and the demand is growing fast. And there are rumors that they're getting ready to sell a version that works on humans, too."

Tanyith shook his head. "That's all bad."

"It is. Diana says the local authorities are aware but there's not all that much they can do beyond the usual."

"I imagine they'll use a secure distribution system for the human version, much like they have for the magicals." He'd been present when several of those deals went down, and it had involved people very high up in the gang structure. So high, in fact, that it had been a shock to see them personally linked with the trade. *Maybe that's a way to destroy them—if we can put the police in the right place at the right time.* Even as he thought it, he knew it was too dangerous. The local authorities weren't well-equipped to handle magical threats, which was why the Atlantean gang and others like it had prospered for so long. *And while they try and fail to deal with the magical gangs, the Zatoras take advantage of the opportunity.*

Nylotte shrugged. "Only time will tell on that one."

"How is it that you have better sources of information in my city than I do?"

His companion laughed. "I know people who know people. More importantly, I know people who know people who owe them favors."

"You're talking about Chadrousse," he commented with a chuckle

"Not only him but others like him as well. You meet many different folks in my business and some of them know people in your city."

"Speaking of different folks, what more can you tell me about the black-suited people, the agents who joined us at the docks?"

She leaned back and folded her arms. "Is there something specific you want to know?"

Tanyith sensed suspicion—or maybe it was merely protectiveness—and hurried to explain. "They seem incredibly capable and highly knowledgeable about magical threats. I guess I wondered how they might be able to help us in the future or how we might be able to help them, besides providing a convenient portal location." He'd been surprised and pleased when Zeb had agreed to allow the unexpected arrivals at the docks to use the tavern as a location for transits to the city.

The Drow sighed and ran her fingers through her hair. "The leader is my student. She and her team have kind of a wide mandate to deal with magical trouble wherever it crops up. So far, they've operated mainly in this country and primarily in the Northeast. But their footprint is expanding rapidly. You could help them by continuing to report anything weird to me so I can pass it along. Whether or not they'll be able to help you depends on many factors that are outside of your control and mine. Unless it's something catastrophic, I wouldn't count on their assistance. They're a fairly small unit and have significant challenges to contend with already."

"But if we had a lead, you'd be willing to take it to them?"

"Within reason." She scowled. "I'm not a bloody messenger service."

He smothered a laugh. Initially, he'd totally bought into her projected animosity. But the way her student had laughed at her without retribution at the docks had confirmed his suspicions that it was an act—or at least mostly an act. "Of course. I would certainly try to resolve whatever it was on my own first."

Nylotte shook her head slowly. "Unless it's about the drugs. If you hear anything more about them, definitely let me know. For some reason, that situation worries me."

"Will do."

The conversation lagged as they finished their meal and

they went their separate ways thereafter. Tanyith had hoped for more concrete information and a peek into her perspective on the gang's future plans but chose not to push for it when it hadn't been volunteered. *It might simply be that no one knows. Which means we'll all wind up surprised together.* He sighed and pushed the concern out of his mind. *It's time to track down another ex-gang member. Hopefully, this one won't run.*

CHAPTER EIGHT

Usha leaned back in her oversized bathtub—which was easily capable of holding at least two more people her size—and luxuriated in the hot water and the steam that filled the room. The well-appointed apartment wasn't far from the Shark Nightclub and was in fact owned by the same shadowy corporation that ran the business. Unlike the previous leaders of the Atlantean gang, she thought big and hired big-thinking financial wizards to help her.

This residence was one of many fringe benefits she'd instituted after winning the position of leader. Her wardrobe was another, as was Danna's. *And she'll wind up taking us out of the black and into the red at this rate. That woman is a veritable clothes horse.* She snorted fondly at the thought of her second in command. They'd been partners since the beginning and she trusted no one more, except the Empress herself.

A chill ran through her. *And she's not likely to be all that pleased with me at the moment.* The incident at the docks had been an embarrassment for her and would reflect badly upon her ruler if anyone in New Atlantis took notice and was brave enough to mention it. The former was feasible but the latter far less so. Political machinations with words were rare in the underwater city, as insults tended to be answered with fast and brutal violence. The failure of the enforcers to kill Caliste Leblanc was another negative reflection on her superior since they came from the second tier of the Empress's people.

What I wouldn't give for one of her personal guards for a week. The city would be ours and our enemies absorbed or destroyed. She shook her head to clear the happy vision. *Focus on reality, Usha.*

While her brain was on the line between fantasy and reality, she again took up the idea of converting the girl to their cause. She had proven stronger than expected, and strength was always a virtue in Atlantean culture. Admittedly, she'd need to learn her place, but that was true of all people as they transitioned from young adult to adult and discovered the deeper, faster-moving currents of life. So far, unfortunately, the child was as great an annoyance as her parents had been.

The Leblancs and their private war against anyone who tried to upset the balance of power in the city had been a thorn in her side from the moment she'd arrived on the continent. Alone, the two would have been nothing more than a nuisance, but they had wisely formed connections with most of the magical communities in New Orleans, which gave them access to intelligence and protection they otherwise wouldn't have had.

The Empress had naturally demanded that Usha claw

her way to power in the new city as she had in New Atlantis. She remembered the woman's words distinctly and could picture her standing above and looking down with a soft smile. "If you cannot take power, you do not deserve power. It is better to die trying than to live a life you haven't earned." Killing the Leblancs had been a big step on that path, and she vividly recalled the triumphant sight of them dying at her feet. She took a deep breath and let herself slip beneath the water.

Of all the things in her life, this was her solace. The feeling of being under the surface, the way the sounds changed and the sensation of primal comfort mixed with the instinctive fear of being unable to breathe. Especially, though, the otherworldliness of it, like she'd left all the dingy realities of daily existence behind in trade for a place that would permit a purity of thought. Her brain traveled unfamiliar paths, searching for new solutions to the challenges she faced. After several minutes, she rose, dried herself, and wound her hair in a towel and her body in another before she stepped into the master bedroom.

This, too, was oversized, at least twice as large as any bedroom she'd ever had. Her residence occupied the entire top floor of its building, which had once housed two apartments and some utility space. Now, it was all hers. The bed was king-sized, her walk-in closet enormous, and the antique-white dressing table that was her destination was bigger than her office desk. There, she focused on business. Here, she indulged her desires, within reason. No one but her and her cleaning staff had access, and the workers had been carefully vetted and given the impression that an actress lived there. She sat and retrieved the variety of skin-care products that made up her evening routine. Her phone rang and with a small smile, she tapped the button to put Danna on speaker. "Yes?"

Her second's voice was flat and businesslike, which suggested that she wasn't alone. Usha was sure she was the only person who knew the real Danna, who was as capable of laughing and joking as anyone. But the woman's projected image was all serious, all the time. "There have been no problems with the Zarcanum deliveries to our magical clients. We're still on target to start distributing the new drug to the humans tonight. I'll check on the initial push personally."

"Excellent. Do you anticipate trouble getting the Shine into their hands?" Entrusting something so important to the gang's future to Danna made her uneasy, but at the Empress's urging, she tried to be a little more hands-off in the day-to-day responsibilities so she could focus on the bigger picture. *Including the rebellious redhead who takes after her parents and is becoming as big a nuisance as they were.*

"It's doubtful. But it's good to keep an eye on things when they're starting out."

"I couldn't agree more. What news of our alleged champions?"

The other woman gave a dismissive chuckle. "Alas, they were unable to rise above their failures."

She sighed. The enforcer had seemed like he would be useful, and the witch had been part of the group for some time and had shown promise. But the proscribed punishment for failure was to fight each other to the death, from which the victor would emerge with a clean slate and the loser ascribed the blame for the lack of success. Her second's words meant that whoever had won had been too injured to survive, so both were lost. She shrugged. *It is our way. And perhaps it will inspire those who face the girl next to greater efforts.*

"Do we have adequate replacements for the third bout?" When Danna hesitated, she added, "No. Not you. Not yet."

The other woman made a sound somewhere between a laugh and a growl. "As you wish. I'll find better champions, even if I have to portal to New Atlantis to do it."

"Excellent. Text me when the night's activities are done and let me know they went well."

"Will do. Goodnight."

Usha clicked the end button and pulled the towel off her head as she picked her brush up. She found that particular self-care chore soothing and needed something positive to shrug off the dirt of her underlings' failures. Like her lack of success shaded her superior, theirs soiled her. She would have to find a way to atone, and one idea returned constantly to the front of her mind.

How can I convince the girl to join us? A second thought emerged unexpectedly. *Or how can I force the girl to join us?*

Rion Grisham held court each evening in a different restaurant and varied his choices and schedule so no enemies could predict where he might be on any given night. He was treated like a king in each, though, and his lieutenants delivered threats and promises as needed to ensure he would be afforded every luxury the venue could provide. Tonight, it was Carlyle's Bistro, an Italian restaurant on Decatur a few blocks away from the touristy areas. The main area was all glass and metal, with small candles on the tables and romantic seating all around.

The back room held only the gang leader and his closest comrades. Even his girlfriend of the moment was unwelcome and spent her time at the bar in the main room as he'd ordered her to do. They sat around a table that could have seated six, with Grisham at the head, his two human lieutenants on his left, and his magic man on the right. Tonight, the wizard was in his usual disguise—probably due to the presence of the others—which was welcome. His tendency to use his powers for trivial things, generally at his boss' expense, rubbed him the wrong way. However, since he didn't have a replacement handy, it was something he'd decided to simply accept. *For now, anyway.*

In front of them rested plates of pasta, glasses of wine, and baskets of bread with small dishes of oil and balsamic. The owner, a portly man in a fine suit, stood in the shadows nearby. The mage had raised a sight and sound shield that would prevent him from hearing their words or reading their lips, which he lifted only when they needed something from the restaurant.

The thinner of his human helpers was closest and dabbed sauce from his mouth with the cloth napkin before he set it aside. Colin Todd was clean-shaven and wore a suit and tie as always, following the example of his boss. His brown-blonde hair hung to his collar and no lower, and his face was perfectly ordinary. He wouldn't have looked out of place behind a pharmacy counter, merely a little overdressed. "So, boss, the word around town is that the 'Lants are bringing a new product to the streets in addition to the one for magicals. A drug for humans."

Grisham frowned. He'd heard the rumors, certainly, but the reality had materialized faster than expected. "Have we managed to get any?"

The bigger man, Jack Strang, played the role of muscle when he needed it but was much more capable than that. He'd been a linebacker in high school and might have gone pro if he hadn't become involved in a betting ring in his first year at college. His suit was too big and he hated ties but otherwise, he was a handsome giant. He shook his bald head. "Not yet. So far, it's only words. But there haven't been as many of the bastards out on the streets today. They might be gearing up for something."

"Like what?"

The slender man took control of the conversation again. "My bet is they're rolling out the new product. It's the only thing that makes sense. They wouldn't be stupid enough to try to attack us. Not after the last time."

Grisham took a bite of the Farfalle Bolognese in front of him and chewed thoughtfully, then chased it with a deep drink of the entirely pedestrian Chianti that was the best the place had to offer. Even though he'd become accustomed to the finer things in life, he hadn't left his roots behind. At his core, he was a street rat made good, and nights like tonight kept him grounded. "So. What do you suggest we do about it?"

The mage was the first to reply. "Kill them all." Three heads turned toward him, and he shrugged. "What? Why should we be afraid of them? If they're moving in on our territory, we should make sure they discover real fast exactly why it's a bad idea." Ozahl's words were always at odds with his almost boring presence. Tonight, he was in a polo shirt and khakis, neither of which seemed to fit well. *Brown hair, brown eyes, and dull as dirt. But he's as smart as hell and deceptively vicious.*

The slim man leaned back and folded his arms. "Isn't that a little...uh, provocative? We don't want an all-out war, here."

He shrugged. "Neither do they, which is what makes the strategy work. If we push, they'll get mad and consider countering but will realize the only real options are to back off or match us at street level. But we have the advantage. We know we're already at war, even if it's a secret one. If they attack us, we'll eliminate those people, too."

Grisham's human lieutenants swiveled their heads toward him, clearly unwilling to move ahead without first gaining a sense of his perspective. He remained silent and nodded for them to continue. Strang shrugged and cracked his knuckles. "I'm not against using the opportunity. They'll be focused on doing their deals and we can hunt them in packs. We can find the outliers, attack them when they don't expect it, kill them, and take their merchandise."

The mage extended a hand toward the other man with his palm up as if to say, "See? He gets it." The gang leader tapped his fingers on the table. "If it blows up, are we strong enough to win?" He had his own opinion on the answer but was always interested to know what those closer to the action might think.

The men on his left both nodded but unexpectedly, Ozahl shook his head and spoke. "No. If it goes to full, all-out war, their magic will provide an edge that we can't match no matter how many guns or soldiers you can bring to reinforce you. But it won't go that far. They're not ready."

"How do you know?" Todd asked.

The mage smiled. "I have my sources."

"And you trust these sources enough to bet your life on their information?" he demanded.

His pet wizard nodded. "Completely. Believe me, the Atlanteans are still getting their ducks in a row. In a few weeks from now, my answer might be different. But tonight, as long as we're careful, we can act without worry that we might draw any retribution we can't handle."

Grisham considered the options. His patience for the situation had worn thin, and his people had taken a few losses at the Atlanteans' hands lately, both at the holding facility and at the docks. A little revenge would feel good personally and more importantly, would look good for the Zatoras as a whole. *So, let's do it.*

He pointed at the men on his left. "You two spread the word. Have our people watch for theirs and report to Ozahl when they see them. Also, warn them to be on the alert for counterattacks." They nodded, and he turned to the mage. "You gather a couple of troops and get out there. Take out as many as you can without pushing it to the point of forcing a reaction. Let's be quiet and conservative on this one. And definitely bring back a sample of the new stuff they're peddling. We need to find a way to compete."

His magic man smiled. "As you wish, boss."

The owner bustled forward to refill his glass while his men all stood and headed to the door. He watched them leave and shook his head at their departing backs.

We may not want an all-out gang war and they may not be ready, but neither of those things guarantees that one isn't about to start. He finished his wine and rose to find his girlfriend of the moment. *So we'll party tonight, for tomorrow, we might die.*

CHAPTER NINE

Ozahl walked into one of the trendy clubs the Zatora soldiers frequented and circulated through the room in search of individuals he considered at least moderately reliable to join him on the night's adventure. He'd donned a dark overcoat that covered him from shoulders to ankles that he liked much more than the rest of his outfit. *But one must keep up appearances.*

He noticed two of his favorites quickly, a man and a woman who could almost always be found together. They were imports from New York City, and he'd endeavored to create a working relationship with them immediately after they'd arrived a year before. The chances of them being connected to people in town who might cause him trouble were remote since they were newcomers, and that made them an ideal choice for his needs.

The duo was drinking together at a table with a gaggle of other Zatora people and a few civilian groupies around them. They didn't have a romantic relationship and hadn't yet engaged in any within the gang, according to all the information he could discover. *Which, to be fair, is considerable.* They would quickly be crossed off his list of associates if they found a special connection with anyone other than one another for fear that they might be influenced. But for now, they seemed to be enjoying themselves without concern for anything other than increasing their value to the organization and satisfying whatever desire pushed them at any given moment.

The mage stepped up to the table and caught their attention. "Hey, you two. I have a task from the boss. Do you want to come along?"

They responded exactly as expected, pushed the other people out of the way, and climbed out of the semicircular booth behind the table. Lila came first, her long blonde hair hanging in braids over her brown suede jacket. "You know it," she replied and smoothed the legs of her leather pants. Dalton stood a moment later and answered with a nod. He played businessman tonight and wore corporate casual khakis and a button-down dress shirt. He'd claimed once before that it appealed to the kind of women he liked, and Ozahl had stopped him from sharing more.

"Good." He turned and headed to the exit, confident that they would follow him. His mind was already considering the next steps. When they reached the street, he turned and strode toward the location where he expected the Atlanteans would begin their distribution. It had taken a fair amount of internal deliberation to decide which of the several potential options would be the most likely and in the end, he selected the one that offered the easiest repositioning in case he'd misjudged.

They arrived at the target block, which was filled with a number of seedy bars. It was mainly a destination for locals, rather than tourists. He was positive the Atlanteans were interested in more than simply making money from the trade, which made a focus on the city's visitors less likely. *No, they're up to something else.* He remembered being told that everything the gang did served their larger plan, and that was doubtless still the case.

Ozahl drew his associates into the shadows when he recognized two Atlantean street soldiers meandering down the sidewalk. He couldn't see their faces under the low-tilted ball caps they wore, and their baggy jeans and sweatshirts might conceal any number of weapons. Quickly, he cast a subtle veil, an increase of shadow that would break up their outlines. Against humans, he would have done more, but the problem with battling magicals was that they could often sense enemy magic nearby. It required walking a fine line to use enough to gain an advantage but not enough to lose anonymity. The cadence of their shuffling footsteps didn't change, which suggested that his effort had been successful.

"They're the muscle," he whispered. We need to wait for the dealers."

His allies were too professional to risk discovery with a reply, which was another reason he preferred to work with them. A group of revelers stumbled out of a nearby bar, and the remainder of the enemy crew materialized. The one who held the product emerged from the shadows across the street and the money man slid out of hiding farther down the sidewalk from them. The soldiers watched the transaction without being obvious about it, and a fifth person appeared to make the delivery after the cash changed hands. He shook his head. "Five. We'll have to go hard and fast. Our first priority is to snatch the drugs. The second is the cash. Third is to make sure they are all incapacitated—preferably permanently. If one gets away and it's safe to do so, we pursue them so they can't warn the others."

The man chuckled quietly. "And the more we get, the more we make, right?"

He nodded. "Same as always." They perked up at his words because one of the things that kept them loyal and willing to go with him at a moment's notice was that he didn't take a cut for himself. He had many ways to obtain money and allowing them to enjoy the earnings from the tasks he needed to accomplish to stay in Grisham's good graces was an easy sacrifice that paid huge dividends. "I'll disable the holder. You two target the delivery boy and the cash man. The soldiers will want to fight rather than run, so if we strike fast enough, we can deal with them all with minimum effort."

Quiet rustles beside him announced that his soldiers drew their weapons. Lila produced two blades. A punch dagger appeared in her left hand and a foldout knife for slashing in her right. Dalton slipped brass knuckles over his right hand and with his left, grasped a heavy sap that he usually carried at the small of his back. He always took the left side and her the right, so their dominant hands were apart, a sign of their intelligence and martial aptitude.

Ozahl waited until the group started another sale before he hissed, "Go." He hurried across the street and hoped he'd make it all the way before the guards decided to check their surroundings again. Fortunately, the new customer was an attractive woman in a short dress, which seemed to hold their attention. He reached the alley and the man who stood there stiffened in surprise and demanded, "What the hell are you doing?"

The mage grinned and gestured with his hand. A surge of force lifted the Atlantean and hurled him sideways into the brick wall beside him. He fell, dazed, and Ozahl collected the tiny marked packages from where they'd fallen to the pavement and shoved them into the pockets of his overcoat. A squeeze of his fist summoned magic that began to choke his foe, and he continued to apply pressure while he turned to watch his cohorts engage their targets.

They had raced past the guards, who lurched into motion to follow them but were still several seconds behind. Lila chose the one with the cash, a dark-skinned Atlantean in the standard jeans and hoodie combination. He had no chance to resist when she bounded up to him and punched him in the stomach with her left hand. The short blade stabbed into him and as he grunted, she slashed with the other hand to slice deep wounds in his protecting arms. He howled and fell and she searched his pockets quickly. She shoved what she found into her own as she turned toward their remaining opponents.

Dalton's quarry saw him coming and tried to angle away. A sprint brought him in range, and the sap whipped in a short arc and caught the opposing gang member in the temple. The Atlantean fell without a murmur. His attacker searched the man's pockets and claimed what he discovered.

By then, the guards had closed and one gravitated to

each threat. Ozahl had feared they'd draw guns, but they were wiser than that. So far, the skirmish hadn't drawn much attention, so they probably thought they could finish it quickly and get on with their night, not realizing how formidable those who had attacked them were. He considered blasting them but decided to conserve his power and enjoy the show instead.

His henchman met them first and he chopped a short block as the Atlantean whipped a haymaker at his face. He intercepted it with ease and the guard followed up with a shuffle inward and jab to the midsection that Dalton took with a laugh. He evaded the follow-up straight punch, and when his adversary threw a hook with his left, it was halted by a blow to his forearm with the brass knuckles. Even though Ozahl couldn't hear the snap over the sounds of the wind, the strange angle his lower arm assumed and his shriek of pain told the tale. The distraction cost him as his attacker whipped the sap up between the guard's legs, then struck at his head as he bent in agony. He toppled, unconscious at the very least.

By then, Lila had engaged her opponent. This man had brought a toy of his own, a large knife he produced from somewhere under his dark sweatshirt. He slashed horizontally, then flicked the blade in a surprise backhand. She avoided both strikes with quick shifts of her weight and snapped a kick at his midsection. He blocked and brought his off-hand down hard enough to make her lurch forward. Ozahl was fairly sure he saw the man grin as he lifted the knife high and plunged it down at her spine.

Her stumble had been a ruse, however. She dropped flat

to avoid the attack and thrust her knife through his sneaker into the top of his foot. The Atlantean howled in pain as she yanked the blade out and stabbed it into his other shoe. He fell and she kicked the weapon out of his hand. She bent toward his face and when he tried to raise an arm to stop her, she jabbed the limb with her small blade. Ozahl couldn't hear her, but he was adept at reading lips. Lila said, "Remember how it feels to lose," and flicked her main blade to slice his cheek. She straightened and headed over to the mage, joined on the way by her partner. When they arrived, she asked, "Should we finish them?"

He detected the faint sound of a siren and shook his head. They'd fulfilled their most important objectives, although he would have preferred to actually kill them. "No, we've done what we need to do here. Let's find another group in a less public location and you can take them off the board permanently." The bloodthirsty grins on their faces confirmed that, once again, he'd chosen the right support for his mission.

When Ozahl reached his apartment, he carefully deactivated the wards that protected the space in his absence. It had been the work of many days to create them, placing an obvious layer over a less obvious one, and a truly devious one beneath. He was sure it was impossible for anyone other than him to get through them unless he permitted it.

The entry opened onto the living room, which held two comfortable couches covered in even more comfortable pillows set at a right angle to one another. A dark wood coffee table stood between them with a metal holder supporting three pillar candles in the center. A whisper and a pointed finger lit each, the magical energy channeled through the wooden rings he wore that were obvious enough to cause most to judge them some kind of strange wand that allowed him to cast.

Most would be wrong, however. They were a misdirection, as was his entire persona. Only here, with his publicly carried phone carefully locked away in a box that prevented it from sending or receiving signals, could he truly be himself. With a sigh, he stretched his arms high and let the illusion fall. His height remained constant as the fifteen pounds of extra flesh he pretended to have evaporated and left a slim man in its wake. The messy brown hairstyle he'd adopted morphed into a well-styled shining black, and his skin became paler as the tan he affected vanished. His eyes changed color from dull brown to a stunning blue that bordered on turquoise. He wandered down the hall and washed his face, another part of his ritual for clearing the other personality out of his mind for a time.

The person in the mirror wasn't a wizard and in fact, wasn't from Oriceran at all. He was a pale-skinned half-Atlantean, the product of a mixed marriage involving a human. Most of her mother's looks except the eyes had come to him along with all his father's magic. His true self grinned at him before he turned and headed down the hallway. When he entered the bedroom, Danna Cudon looked at him from where she sprawled on the bed, her normal suit traded for skimpy shorts and a skimpier t-shirt. She smiled widely. "How was work, love?"

He let a long, deep kiss serve as the first part of the answer, and by the time they surfaced for breath, they'd both forgotten the question.

CHAPTER TEN

Cali had stayed in bed all day Tuesday to allow herself to heal and rose only to wrangle food for herself and Fyre. In truth, the amount the Draksa ate was one of the most surprising things about him. Some days, it amounted to nothing. Other days, he seemed to eat his own weight in fish and meat. She guessed it was some generational adaptation for the species, but when she thought to ask during one of her lucid moments while awake the day before, he'd simply given her his most annoying smile and replied "Look it up. You know, at the library."

She'd forced herself up with a groan that morning and arrived at the dojo in time to do her chores there before her training session with Ikehara. Her whole body seemed to drag and she had barely managed the energy to put on her least dirty shorts and a t-shirt. Of course, her teacher noticed her sluggishness as she went through the warmup forms and questioned her. They'd spent half their time together with her sharing details about the fight and him offering comments and critiques about her decisions.

Everything is a teaching opportunity for this guy. She was glad for the instruction but relieved when the debrief ended, as there were apparently many different choices she could have made that would have improved the outcome. She knew it all came from the best of intentions but was still a little raw over the injuries she'd sustained. Even if he hadn't chided her for it, she would have chided herself.

She stood opposite him with her magical sticks in her hands and waited for his command to begin. He lifted training knives in his fists, shifted his feet into a fighting stance, and nodded. She darted in quickly, then side-stepped to circle him. The feint failed to draw him out and he turned with her. *It was worth a try. Let's see how he likes this.* She stepped in far enough to reach him and swung both sticks from their guard positions in simultaneous outside-in strikes aimed at his temple and his elbow.

Her expectation that he'd retreat was thwarted when he stepped toward her. He raised his left arm in a block against her right wrist, stopped the weapon aimed at his head, and accepted the other's impact against his right elbow, which was too weak to damage him because of his altered position. The right knife stabbed at her stomach, and she stepped around with her back foot to turn perpendicular and allow it to pass in front of her. She let the left stick fall from her grasp and attempted a lock. As her fingers closed on his wrist, he tried to twist the knife to cut her but she bent the joint in such a way that it locked with the sharp edge of the blade away from her.

She had many options from that position but selected the one she liked best and yanked him forward. He stumbled, and she recognized it for the trap it was in the instant before he spun and lanced his left-hand knife at her head. She pivoted as well and blocked it with her right stick. For a moment, they stood back to back before he made a deft twist to free himself from her grasp.

"Stop," he commanded, and she obeyed and assumed a wary but respectful stance across from him. Only once had he followed an order to halt with a follow-up attack, but contrary to Emalia's oft-stated opinion, Cali was actually capable of learning.

Ikehara nodded and approval glinted in his dark eyes. "That was a good response. You didn't let yourself be distracted by the moment. But you've become predictable. Anyone who has watched you fight before knows you'll try that move at some point."

She sighed. *Expillarimus. Exactly like Harry Potter.* He had used the fictional wizard's over-reliance on that spell and how it resulted in disaster as an example before. "Got it. I'll work on it."

"Excellent. So, your reflexes with the sticks have improved dramatically. They are truly an extension of your hands now. Against knives, you will need to better maintain your distance as shorter weapons will limit your responses." She nodded. He'd provided a very concrete example of why she'd have to do that. "What would you like to face next?"

Cali gazed at the weapons wall in thought. Over the last couple of weeks, he'd chosen a weapon for the first part of their training session, then allowed her to select one for the second half. She thought about what she might face, which led her to think about the Atlanteans, which led her to consider the biggest mystery in her life at the moment.

With a small laugh at all the answers she didn't have, she replied, "A single sword."

He clapped his hands together in approval and strode to retrieve the weapon, each step a demonstration of his abundant strength and grace. *If I moved like that, I'd totally have my choice of boyfriends. If I had time for a relationship, that is.* She locked that thought away in her brain and wrapped it in caution tape so it couldn't escape. Her teacher spun the blade through an impressive series of warm-up swings, shifted it from hand to hand, and twirled it around his body.

Ikehara slid seamlessly into a ready stance and she squeezed her sticks and matched him. His bamboo sword was held high, the point angled toward her and his body a straight line that presented the narrowest target. She raised one stick high and positioned the other low, prepared to counter an attack at any height. Typically, she would take the defensive against the larger weapon, but when he started to move, she attacked in a rush. Exactly as he'd done with the knives, she narrowed the distance so her shorter weapons would have an advantage. She flicked the left one toward his head as a distraction and paid for it when the hilt impacted with her hand and made her drop the stick. Her main hand weapon whipped forward at his knee, and although he lifted his shin to take the blow, she knew she could have scored with it against almost any other opponent.

His sword whistled as he chopped down and she maintained momentum into a roll to get behind him. He had already swung as she stood, but she blocked it easily and called her magic weapon to her hand. She whipped it at his face and he was forced to release the sword with one hand to intercept it. A quick loop with her other one positioned it for a strike at his fist and he dropped his weapon. She stepped back quickly to end the round.

A wide smile spread over his features. "Good. You made some changes there. Well done. Between now and our next session, consider what moves you use too often and how you can modify or replace them. You won't disarm me so easily again, that I promise you."

Easy? You call that easy? She shook her head and laughed. "Whatever you say, Sensei."

He nodded with a playful glint in his eye. "As it should be. Now, get ready for class."

After the class, Cali portaled home for a shower since Ikehara had decided that everyone "looked tired and needed to sweat." The blissfully hot water that cascaded over her was a luxury she never wanted to leave but after ten minutes, she ran out of time. She dried her hair, put on her favorite jeans and a Led Zeppelin t-shirt, and nudged Fyre into motion. The walk to Emalia's lasted most of a half-hour and brought them there precisely when she was supposed to arrive. A closed sign hung on the door but it was unlocked, and they passed through into the small room at the back.

The tea was already waiting and appealing notes of cinnamon and apple floated through the air. She sat, took a few delightful sips, and sighed happily. "Now that is a good brew." The Draksa sniffed and made a pleased noise, then curled under the table.

Her great aunt had apparently decided not to tell fortunes that day as she was in her casual clothes, a long skirt under a button-down shirt and oversized cardigan. She laughed at Cali's reaction. "You kids today are soft. When I was young, we drank bitter tea and we liked it."

"Made from roots you harvested from dying trees on the way to a fourteen-hour shift simultaneously working in a factory and going to school. Yes, I know the story." She grinned.

The older woman continued to laugh, then wiped her eyes. "The mouth on you, child. You remind me of your mother more every day." Some memory caused her to frown slightly, and she pushed it away with a visible effort. "So. You were in another fight." Before doing her Rip Van Winkle imitation, Cali had called everyone to update them on the event and her reasonable health.

"I did. And now, I have two weeks before I have to worry about the next one."

"Which will be three-on-three." That she knew the rules of Atlantean ritual combat shouldn't have been a surprise and yet it was, merely another in a long line of unexpected talents revealed by her great aunt.

Cali finished her tea and held the cup out for more. "Yes."

As she poured, Emalia asked, "Who will you choose as your third?"

The question was unexpected, and she chided herself internally for not having thought about it already. "I guess I don't have many options. Tanyith, I suppose."

The woman nodded. "You might want to get Zeb to ask the council for help beyond that. Your list of direct allies is frightfully small and I'd prefer not to have to take the field myself. I'm a little old for such things." The soft smile told her she would do so in an instant if necessary.

No way can I allow that to happen. "Will do."

"So, I think it's time to change the direction of your training for a while. What you've learned so far should serve you in most subtle situations, but we need to prepare you for the coming battle and the ones after that." She paused, then added, "You know, you really should read up on the rituals."

She sighed, stood, and stretched her arms wide and twisted them to loosen tired muscles. "At the magical library, yes, I'm fully aware. I'm going there in the next couple of days. Let it go, woman." Emalia rose with a laugh and summoned a portal. On the other side was a large, dark, open space she didn't recognize, but she stepped through without worry, knowing her mentor would never, ever lead her astray. Fyre followed on her heels and the older woman did as well before she closed the rift behind them.

They were in an empty warehouse judging by the large doors along one wall and the numerous scuffs on the floor that made a grid shape suggesting pallets and forklifts. The amount of dust lingering in the air and rising from the ground with each step indicated that it hadn't been used in some time. She whipped around as a thought occurred to her. "This isn't 1601, is it?"

Emalia shook her head. "No, child, no such luck. I'm sorry. This is merely a place that...a friend owns."

Cali folded her arms and regarded her with a grin. "Invel."

The older woman blushed enough for it to be detectable. "Perhaps. But that's irrelevant. We are here to work on your skills." She made a complex series of gestures and said words she couldn't make out, and a translucent target appeared about twenty feet away. It was humanoid and resembled an enforcer, stocky and tall. "Show me your force magic."

She obliged and punched the air and the image rippled where the magic struck. When she turned to her teacher in expectation of approval, she received only a slight frown.

"Can you do it without punching? Point and fire?" She demonstrated with a raised hand and the air itself rippled as a blast of magical force crossed the distance to the illusory enemy.

The girl frowned and concentrated, raised a palm, and willed the power to flow. When it didn't, her expression transformed into a scowl, and she searched her brain for a way to make it happen. The image of a stormtrooper from Star Wars slipped into her mind, and she pictured the energy as a blaster bolt. A burst of force leapt from her hand to drive into the target with enough power to make it vanish for a second. She turned to Emalia with wide eyes.

Her teacher nodded. "Yes. Exactly that. You chose the paths that worked best when your magic was restricted, but now that it is free, there are better ways to use it."

"Could I channel that into a punch like I used to?"

She shrugged. "Doubtless, with enough practice. Now, I want you to imagine your pool of magic as lava."

Cali closed her eyes and visualized the heart of a

volcano roiling within her. It took her almost a minute before she felt like she could sustain it in the face of distractions. When she opened her eyes, Emalia pointed at the target. "The idea is the same. Send fire from your hands to the target."

Fear coiled around her mind. She'd never been comfortable with that form of magic, a fact her great aunt was well aware of. Despite her misgivings, she took a deep breath and pushed but nothing emerged.

"Don't force it," her mentor whispered. "Release it and simply let it flow." She nodded and adjusted her thinking to imagine a line extending from her hand to the enforcer illusion like a candle wick. With that in place, she focused her entire being on the idea of flames racing down it. The power erupted from her almost instantly, seared across the intervening space, and engulfed the target. Unfortunately, it also spread about ten feet in every direction and several small fires started when piles of debris ignited.

Fyre responded in an instant. He immediately became airborne and swooped to bathe the area with his frost breath. For good measure—or simply fun—he rolled like an old-school biplane and coated the target as well, then flew through it with his claws extended in a show of Draksa martial prowess. Both women laughed at the display, and the dragon lizard made a few more rolls in the air before he landed beside her with a strong flap of his wings and folded them primly along his body.

Her great aunt shook her head. "So, control is an issue. Under the circumstances, we probably shouldn't practice fire anywhere other than here."

Cali laughed. "So, no showing off at the tavern?"

"I think Zeb would be upset if you incinerated his guests. Or his furniture."

She nodded. "Yeah, that's probably true. Depending on the guest, of course."

The older woman put her hand on her shoulder. "You did very well today. Changing your use of force and accessing new magic is no small feat. You have what it takes to be a devastatingly powerful sorcerer."

As they stepped through the portal, the statement she knew was inevitable was finally delivered. "You know, you could probably learn about how to do magic at the library. Perhaps you've heard of it?"

CHAPTER ELEVEN

Tanyith pushed through the door of the Drunken Dragons, careful not to let it slam against the wall, and took his usual seat with its back to the entrance and nearest Zeb's custom brew. The dwarf pulled him a tall glass, which turned out to be a delicious mulled cider. He'd learned the hard way that the cask tended to be far more potent than most of the other offerings at the tavern, and this was no exception.

They chatted for a minute before the bartender stepped away to exchange words with the annoyed redhead who'd bounded up from the common room. Cali looked physically none the worse for wear after her fight against the Atlanteans, but he imagined it might nag at her mind. *Or she's simply irritated because customers are sometimes the worst kind of people.* He laughed. *Me included.*

His reverie was interrupted when a heavy hand settled on his shoulder. "Hey, Shale, what's up?"

Without looking back, he replied, "Not a thing, Detective. Are you here for work or pleasure?"

Kendra Barton shrugged as she slid onto the seat closest to him around the curve of the bar's corner. "Work is a pleasure, am I right?" She was definitely off-duty, though, since she wore jeans, a t-shirt, and a motorcycle jacket, none of which he'd seen her wear in her official capacity.

"Not as such. Whatcha drinking?"

"What do you have?"

"Alcoholic rocket fuel with hints of apple, cinnamon, and cardamom."

She laughed. "Can I have a taste?" He slid the glass to her, and she took a sip, then another. "Damn, that's fine stuff. Barkeep," she called and when Zeb looked at her, she pointed at the cask. He nodded, and she shoved the glass to her companion after one last sip. The red-bordering-on-purple shade of her lipstick was stuck to the rim.

He tapped his finger on the bar. "So, technically, you evaded my question rather than answered it."

The woman nodded. "I'm good like that. It's one of my better qualities. Try another."

"Are you here to see me?"

"Not specifically."

"Cali?"

Barton turned to look at the common room and her head tracked the girl's movements for a few moments before she turned back. "Not specifically."

"Zeb then."

She laughed. "As a bartender, very specifically." Her glass appeared before her and she drank a third of it quickly.

"Okay, so you're suffusing yourself with the magical community, I get it."

"What are you doing, question man? Have you found a job yet? Or are you still playing at PI?" She leaned an arm on the bar and twisted toward him. Her dark eyes were piercing, which was doubtless an advantage in her line of work.

"I'm not playing. I'm private and I'm investigating. It's work." *Work that isn't going particularly well at the moment.* "Chasing down leads." *Literally.* "Putting the pieces together." *Hah. If only they'd fit.* "You know how it is."

The woman drained another third of her drink. "I do indeed know how that game is played."

Tanyith scowled to cover his enjoyment of the banter. "Not. Playing."

"Right. I forgot. Sorry. Hey, maybe you should get a Sherlock Holmes hat and one of those big magnifying glasses."

"He was a detective, Detective. Perhaps you should."

She laughed. "You might be right. I could totally rock that look." She leaned closer to him. "Okay, for real, I did come here for a drink, but I also kind of hoped I'd run into you three. Caliste seems busy, so you'll do." She dipped a hand into the pocket of her jacket and slid a small waxy package to him. A faintly glowing blue powder rested inside and a red symbol appeared on the front. It looked like a shooting star or something.

He shifted his gaze to meet hers. "Is this what I think it is?"

The detective nodded. "It's a new drug on the streets aimed at humans and distributed by Atlanteans. They call it Shine."

He turned it in his hands, careful to hide it from outside view. "Holy hell. That can't be good."

"The people on the drug enforcement side of the house shared it with me. They think it's merely more of the same. But, given what y'all have been involved in recently, I have some serious doubts about that."

"Me too." He thought about the implications. "They must be trying to cut into the Zatoras revenue, at least."

"Yeah, and they don't seem to be too happy about it. There were beatings and a couple of killings of Atlantean gang members. They didn't have any drugs on them but it wasn't too hard to put two and two together."

Tanyith caught Zeb's eye and gestured for another round while he considered what she'd told him. "What do you think the Atlanteans are up to?"

"You're the one with the inside track."

He sighed. "I'm honestly not sure if you're merely bashing me for no good reason or if you believe it."

She finished her drink and leaned closer. "It's the first one. I've had people watching you so I know you're clean. At the moment, anyway." She returned to her previous pose and sipped her second glass.

"So. Quit dodging and answer the damn question, then."

"Okay." Barton laughed. "There are a number of possibilities, any or all of which could be true based on my long experience with criminal organizations." She counted them on her fingers. "One, it's only a money-making ploy. Everyone needs money, especially those who need to show flash and success in order to stay in power."

"That's a given. Even stupid people like me could have come up with that one."

"Two. It's a deliberate strike against the Zatoras' ability to make money for the same reasons in reverse. It would make them look bad and weaken the leader."

"Okay, I can see that. When do we get to the part where your vast knowledge of criminal organizations comes into play?"

The woman stuck out her tongue at him, which probably didn't achieve the effect she was going for since it made her seem less professional and more fun. "Three—and here's where the scary stuff starts—it's a deliberate effort to weaken the humans in the city through drug addiction. We'll know more about that when we get the tests back and have an idea about how potent it is."

That possibility hadn't occurred to him and the potential danger left him speechless for a moment. When he could make words happen again, he asked, "How likely is that? And how long before you have the results?"

Barton shrugged. "There's no way to tell how depraved these bastards might be. We gotta plan for the worst. And hopefully tomorrow, maybe the next day. It's fast-tracked, but the lab is busy, as always."

"It must be hard putting yourself in that headspace." He didn't know the comment was coming until it was already out, and the look of pain that flickered across her face was equally unexpected.

She sipped her drink before she replied. "It can be but it comes with the territory." She sighed. "And we haven't even reached the worst one yet." She lifted four fingers. "What if it's a delayed poison? They could be out to kill everyone who's not a magical."

The shock of her words left him momentarily woozy. "That's...insane."

The detective nodded. "Yep. There are many crazies out there, though. Mind you, that's worst-worst-case and unlikely."

"What would you do if it turned out to be true?"

Her laugh was brittle. "Call in the National Guard, quit my job, and move to Kansas to become a corn farmer." The image of her on a tractor in a straw hat surfaced, and he choked on the sip of cider he'd taken. She slapped him on the back several times before he regained his composure and raised an eyebrow at him. "Are you all right over there?"

He nodded and his eyes watered. His voice was hoarse, unfortunately not in the leading man sexy kind of way. "Yeah. You. A farmer. Not likely."

"I agree. So let's hope option four doesn't happen. Okay, tell me about your alleged job."

"That will require a third round. Maybe something a little less potent, though." Zeb was in earshot and delivered a winter lager from one of the local breweries. It complemented the cider, which proved once again that the dwarf knew his brews. Barton nodded in satisfaction after a sip. "So, I've been hired to find a guy who seems to have vanished into thin air."

"By who?"

"An old friend. It's not important. I've gone through all the people I know from the past who are still around. I track them, watch them for a while to make sure they're not connected to the gang anymore, then have a chat with them. By now, I've talked to more than a dozen and a half and only a couple have had anything useful to share." It was mostly the truth, although Dray's connection to the gang activity in town retained an open question mark. The other man had been out of touch since their last meeting, and part of Tanyith worried about what he'd landed himself in by pretending to be interested in joining his team.

"So, you're saying you've also identified some who are still with the gang?"

He shook his head. *The woman is always working.* "I guess I have."

She leaned forward so they wouldn't be overheard, even though the only one close enough to do so was Zeb or maybe Cali as she hurried past on the way to retrieve drinks. "Do you care to share?"

"You don't quit, do you?"

Barton laughed. "Never."

Tanyith took a deep breath and looked her squarely in the eyes. "What's it worth to you?"

An elegant eyebrow raised in response. "If you rub my back, I'll rub yours."

A million flirty answers came and went in an instant, and he selected none of them. "Do you have access to police records on your phone?"

"Sure. We're not complete Luddites."

"Will you look someone up for me and forget about them?"

Without hesitation, she slid her hand into the inner pocket of her jacket and pulled a cell phone out. It was in a heavy black case with the NOPD logo on it. She set it on the bar so he could watch as she swiped to wake it, put her finger in a box that appeared on the screen, and entered an eight-digit code. In silence, she swiped through apps until she found the one she wanted, and when she tapped it, had to enter another numerical password. Finally, she said, "Okay, who's the person?"

He sighed. "I notice you didn't actually commit to forgetting about them."

She gave him a smile that would have looked right on a movie star. *Damn, no more drinking for you.* He pushed his glass away. Barton gestured toward the phone. "Are we simply gonna dance all night, or will you make your move?"

"Try Adam Harlan." He assumed the odds of the alias being in the system might be greater than the man's real name. Or maybe he was still somehow trying to protect Sienna from the truth about her ex-boyfriend. *Either way, I'm probably an idiot.*

She typed it in and data scrolled on the device. "Okay, Adam Harlan. He was picked up several times for small stuff, including drug use but not dealing, and it looks like five arrests but no convictions. He's a handsome fellow." She held the phone up to display a mugshot that had captured him with dirty and tousled hair and a drugged expression. She returned to looking through the information. "Gang affiliations—oh, look, he was part of your old crew. Imagine that."

"Yeah, yeah, get on with it."

"It says here he was also a person of interest in investigations with several other gangs, both magical and not. Your boy got around."

"Why do you say that in the past tense?"

Her expression remained blank. "His records end about seven months ago."

"Damn it." He thumped his fist on the bar in frustration a little more powerfully than intended. "Can you try Harry? Harry Harlan maybe? It was a nickname."

She stared at the record, then typed in a few words. "I'm updating the known aliases for Adam. Okay, let's see what the new search brings." Her eyes widened as the data scrolled. "There's considerable chatter about a Harry, sometimes also using the word Harlan." She looked at him. "Everyone's looking for this guy, and not to shake his hand."

"Including the police?"

Barton nodded. "Yeah. He's into some stuff, man." She turned the phone so he could see the details and he gaped in surprise. Murder was at the top of the list, and not only a single charge. "Shale—Tanyith, what the hell have you gotten yourself into?"

He shook his head in disbelief. "I really don't know."

She snaked a hand out to catch his wrist. "I'd tell you to stop but somehow, I don't think you're smart enough to listen. So instead, let's go fifty-fifty on this guy. I help you find him and you help me catch him so we can either protect him or put him away, depending on what's actually going on."

The seriousness of her grasp made him abandon the flippant reply that was his brain's first offering. The happy haze of drinking had been banished by the cold shower of the new information about the man he thought he knew. He nodded. "Deal. I'll start tomorrow."

CHAPTER TWELVE

Cali had kept an eye on Tay and Barton at the bar all evening and made up stories about their future lives together as a married couple as she worked the floor of the tavern. The crowd wasn't bad for a Wednesday, all things considered, although an annoying group of drunken, cackling witches in the back corner was downright irritating.

Thoroughly disgusted, she stepped up to the bar and gave their orders to Zeb. "Honestly, if they'd drink something other than daiquiris, I'd probably have at least a little respect for them. But as it is, I think they'll have to be banned forever."

He laughed as he filled the order. "Now, now. Remember, those folks pay your salary."

She snorted. "I can do without that portion."

"Well, I can't. This place costs money to run, you know."

"Yeah, yeah, I'm aware." She stacked the new drinks on her tray. "I couldn't possibly help but be aware, given how much you talk about it." She spun away and headed to the crowd before he mustered a reply. *Lame answer, Cali. Do better.*

The rest of the evening passed in a blur of service activities, trading quips with her boss, and trying to listen in on Tay's conversation. Eventually, Barton left and looked a little unsteady as she crossed to the door. When closing time arrived, Tanyith was still in his seat. He helped with the final cleanup and ushered people out of the bar, then reclaimed his seat as she climbed onto the stool the detective had abandoned. Zeb shot a stream of soda water at Fyre, who was resting behind the bar, and they all laughed as he snapped at it exuberantly. He settled onto his belly and the dwarf lit his pipe and pulled a soft cider for each of them before he sat across the wooden surface from her.

"Good work tonight, Cali." He usually gave her some kind of gruff compliment at the end of the evening. She was sure it was a technique he'd picked up from a management book or something.

"Yeah, it was a decent night, but the bartender has the worst attitude. I wish you'd fire him." *Another lame response. I think my sarcasm generator is broken.* She turned to Tanyith. "So, you and Kendra had quite the conversation. Did you set a date for the wedding? Where will you go on your honeymoon?" *That's a little better but it's still not up to my normal standards. I must be tired. And why am I talking to myself?* She sighed and took a sip of her cider, then focused her sleepy brain on the man across from her.

He rolled his eyes, but his heart wasn't in the banter either. "Yeah, that's right. We're thinking New Atlantis. I hear it's nice this time of year."

Cali laughed. "You'd probably be eaten by a monster

octopus en route or something, the way our luck is running."

Zeb interjected, "Speaking of luck, have you made any progress on your mystery man?"

Tanyith shrugged. "Nothing particularly useful. He's in the system and Barton will run more searches to see what she can dig up. But pinning him down at any particular time or place is difficult, present or past."

She barked a laugh. "So, no more late-night chases through the city?"

He gave a half-smile. "I make no promises. Now, I need to wait for the next thing to break." His expression widened into a grin. "Speaking of break, how's the arm?"

"Fine." She growled in annoyance. "It was nothing a healing potion or two couldn't fix."

"Two? I've never heard of it taking more than one."

"Apparently, I'm special."

The dwarf laughed. "Oh, I'll say you're special. It means the formula isn't quite right for you so you must have something weird going on in your genetics. We'll get it dialed in."

Cali looked at Tanyith. "Did he actually use a science word?"

"Yes, he did."

Zeb sighed. "You know, stereotyping is hurtful. There's considerable science in brewing. Tons."

She raised her gaze. "Don't talk to me about stereotypes until you're not a heavy-drinking dwarf with a battle-ax nearby."

They all shared a laugh at the familiar teasing. Zeb was the first to stop, and he looked uncomfortable when he spoke. "So, I have some information to share with you both. From the council."

"Well, that's an ominous start." A frown immediately settled on her face.

Tanyith nodded. "Seriously."

The proprietor didn't smile, which ratcheted her concern up. "It was my hope that the others would agree to take a more active role against the gangs. But while there is definitely a consensus that a problem exists and must be addressed, the group chose what they felt was the most appropriate and expeditious option."

Her frown deepened. "And that is?"

"Basically, letting the two of you run with it until things get worse."

She slapped her palms on the top of the bar. "Damn it. That's seriously shortsighted. What, they'll take an active interest after we're dead? Cowards." The vehemence that surged through her clearly shocked her companions judging by the looks on their faces but did the same to her. *Okay, chill out, Cali.* "Sorry. It's only…it's stupid."

The other person in the line of fire nodded his agreement. "Did they offer any help at all?"

The dwarf shrugged. "Essentially what they've done so far. Information without restriction and help where it can be done in secret."

Cali growled in frustration. "So, they're worried about getting noticed, is that it? What kind of leaders are they?"

Zeb patted a hand in the air in his long-standing signal that she needed to calm herself. Many customers had prompted a plethora of similar admonitions in the past.

"They're leaders who are afraid their citizens will wind up in the middle of a battle."

She sighed. "Okay, that's legit. But still. This sucks." She shifted her gaze to Tanyith. "Can your girlfriend help us?"

"She. Is not. My Girlfriend." He said it slowly, presumably so she'd understand. *Yeah, that won't happen, buddy.* Now that she had a way to get under his skin so quickly, she wasn't about to abandon it for anything silly like "facts" or "reality."

"Sure, sure. The question stands."

"Maybe. We've agreed to work together on Aiden, so we might be able to do more. But do we really want her involved? The fights you're in and the stuff we've done aren't exactly legal. I'm reasonably sure we've chalked up at least one fatality. It might not be a good idea to have a sworn police officer around us any more than absolutely necessary."

Cali tapped her index finger on the bar and considered his words. While nothing he said was wrong, Detective Barton also seemed like a reasonable person. Mostly. If they were able to keep her at arm's length on the fights—*meaning I can't use her as a backup plan anymore, which probably is a good idea, regardless*—maybe they could at least share information. "Okay. We'll let that ride as is for now. But if you find an opportunity to get any relevant info from her or if you think it's safe to give away something we know, I'd say go for it. The same applies to me, although I would guess you'll be the one she seeks out." She wiggled her eyebrows in case her meaning had been unclear.

He rolled his eyes. "Sure."

She turned to Zeb. "Congratulations. You're now my primary backup plan for trouble. If I call you, can you muster people other than you and Valerie to come and help?"

The dwarf grinned widely and fluffed his beard where it rested on his chest. "In the very unlikely circumstance where me and my lady wouldn't be sufficient, I think I could manage to find some folks. I'll lay the groundwork now. It seems like the council ought to at least be able to commit to having backup on call." She was sure she heard a note of disgust in his voice at the group's behavior, which fit her opinion of them well.

It would suffice, for now, and she nodded. "Is there anything else where they're concerned?"

He shrugged. "The gnomes are worried that the gangs will eventually expand to their doorsteps. A couple of others were behind starting a war immediately. The rest don't feel it's the right time and that things haven't reached the critical moment where action is required."

Tanyith finished his cider and held it out for a refill. "They'll only see that point when it's in the rear-view mirror."

"That statement is sadly accurate, I think." Zeb topped off all their ciders as he continued to speak. "But in their places, we might do the same."

"All the others lead their communities," Cali said. "I guess I always believed you were involved because this is a natural gathering place, but you've never mentioned another dwarf. Are you their leader?"

Zeb laughed. "We're mostly not interested in what the others have to say, and there aren't that many of us here, in the first place. We tend to be loners, except when we get together for a drink or a party. None of us sees the need for a leader, and it's enough for them that at least one dwarf is included in discussions. I don't presume to speak for the rest."

"It's like magical Switzerland here," the man said, "and you're the prime minister."

He grinned. "I prefer to consider myself as a builder of bridges between people. Who takes a percentage as they eat, drink, and connect."

She frowned. "So you're basically a fairy tale troll. Not the Tolkien kind but the live-under-a-bridge kind."

"Trolls have been horribly misrepresented in your culture. Seriously, who would choose to live under a bridge? It's xenophobia, is what it is. The person taxing travel was probably a human in disguise."

"So, since you don't do that, you're what, Robin Hood?"

"Not hardly." He laughed. "Although the idea of robbing the rich to give to the poor has some merit. It merely makes me a convenient go-between."

Cali shook her head. "There is nothing convenient about you."

Tanyith interrupted the banter. "Did they say anything about drugs?"

Zeb frowned. "No. Why?"

"Barton mentioned that the Atlanteans have a new product on the streets—one aimed at humans. Combine that with their magical one, and they're making connections with all kinds of people. She thinks that the chances of it only being about money are very small."

She nodded. "Yeah, they're definitely up to something. They're always up to something."

"So. One more thing to worry about." From the look on the man's face, this one really caused him some concern.

The notion disturbed her as well, and she banished any hint of playfulness from her voice. "Okay, to paraphrase *Bad Boys*, stuff just got real. We have two weeks before the scumbags can force me to fight them again, as long as I don't mess with them. Or, at least, mess with them in a way that they know it's me." Fyre gave a growl of support from behind the bar. "In that time, we need to find out more about the sword, what the situation is with the drugs, and where your ex-girlfriend's ex-boyfriend fits into the situation. You might not want to mention that part to Barton. I bet she gets jealous easily." She couldn't suppress the humor in her voice on the ending.

Tanyith shook his head. "You're gonna keep doing it, aren't you?" She nodded. "I need to go home. Too much time around you starts to melt my brain." He pushed off his seat and wandered out to laughter from her and Zeb.

Cali turned to her boss. "I'll need a third for the next battle. Do you want to bring Valerie out of retirement?"

He shook his head. "You have better options and I have to remain the go-between. But if you need help to find someone, I can do it."

It was the answer she'd expected. "No worries. I'm on it."

"So, will you go to the library tomorrow?"

She sighed, exasperated. "What is it with you people? No, actually—dojo, busking, and classwork tomorrow before I come in here. I'll go to the library on Friday when

I can devote most of the day to it before I report to my uncaring boss for another evening in the alcohol-mines."

He laughed. "Good. It seems like you have your priorities mostly straight. Get out of here."

With a final grin of affection, she headed to the basement and Fyre moved lazily behind her. Even with the guarantee of a couple of weeks of downtime, she didn't want to tempt fate by walking home in the dark with so much going on. She sighed inwardly. *I need to eliminate these bastards so I can get back to my old life.*

CHAPTER THIRTEEN

Tanyith strode into the tourist bar and immediately cringed at the sounds of gleeful visitors spreading their happiness loudly and indiscriminately among their fellow patrons. He'd been glad when Dray had texted him with the location because it hadn't been near his new apartment, which he wanted to keep off the radar from everyone. But meeting in the heart of the French Quarter on a Thursday night carried its own challenges, most of them drunk.

He pushed through the crowd and did his best not to offend as he squeezed through openings that were too small to navigate without touching. Ever careful, he tried to chart a course that didn't force him to rub against anyone of the opposite sex, that being an all too common and neanderthal practice in New Orleans' crowded drinking spots.

His contact waited for him in the back corner as he'd said he would near an opening with a neon sign proclaiming "restrooms" over it. *Quick exit options, most likely. He's still smart and probably more street-savvy than when I knew him.* Dray was an old friend, but the discovery of his presence in a human gang with anti-magical tendencies was a surprise. Like Tanyith, his Atlantean heritage wasn't easily noticed but the situation was, nonetheless, an unexpected twist.

The other man looked thinner than usual, the sharp lines in his face keen enough to cut. He wore an expensive suit with no tie and his shoes shined. He nodded at his approach. "It's good to see you again. Nice work on the other thing."

"That guy was an idiot."

Dray laughed. "Yeah. But as an entrance exam, he was a useful idiot. I've made the case that you should be given the option to join us to those above me. They know about our shared past but I've convinced them you don't care for the old gang any more than I do."

Damn, way to strike to the heart of the matter, dude. He said, "I think I need a little more information about how you wound up in the...what, upper echelon of a human gang?"

The other man laughed. "Yeah, that's quite a tale, to be honest, and much of it isn't relevant. Quick strokes, though —when you were taken away, things went in a direction I didn't support. I spoke up and the wench in charge sent a team to kill me. I decided to act against their interests whenever possible from then on because I'm petty and vengeful, and I did some solo work robbing their people after they'd picked up payoffs, things like that."

Tanyith nodded. That sounded exactly like something the man he'd known would do. "And then?"

He shrugged. "This group noticed what I was doing and asked if I wanted to think a little bigger. We agreed that I'd never have to go up against any magicals other than the Atlanteans and that they'd do the same. It's been good since then. Sure, we have the occasional douchebag recruit who needs his or her prejudices beaten out of them, but the group's commitment to our deal has been solid."

"Wow. It's hard to know what to say to that. Are you allied with the Zatoras?"

"Nope. We're independent."

He shook his head. "Now I'm even more amazed. How have you pulled that off?"

Dray laughed, but his body language conveyed tension. "We're too big to be swallowed easily and too small to be a threat. Also, we work hard to ensure we correctly map the edges of their activity and stay on the outside. When they target someone we've had a relationship with, we fade and find someone else to tap. It's the same with territory. It's a vast city and neither of the two big players is too concerned with the smaller parts."

He frowned as he finished, and Tanyith had the sense something was amiss. "Trouble?"

His companion nodded. "A group of street soldiers trying to avoid notice at the front. It looks like four."

"Atlanteans?"

"The hoodies would suggest so. But the fact that they haven't come in means they're probably not alone."

He looked at him in confusion. "Why?"

The man chuckled. "There's been action on the streets over the last few nights. Both gangs travel in larger numbers and are far more conservative when they make a move. A week ago, they would have sent the four in after me without a thought. That it hasn't happened means they're waiting for something. Or someone." He stiffened. "And they must have arrived. Let's move."

Dray led the way through the opening at the back of the bar, past the restrooms, and to an unmarked door near the rear of the building. It claimed an alarm would sound if it was opened, but he pushed through without a reaction. *Magic, maybe, or cheap and lazy owners.* It led to an alley with an asphalt surface, about eight feet wide and as long as the block. Tanyith peered right and located three men in hoodies who stood and waited. He moved left, only to see two more come from that direction.

His companion muttered curses under his breath. "They seem to have planned this one reasonably well."

"What do you have in mind?"

The man turned, raised his hand, and sent a wide cone of fire at the trio to the right. "Same as always. Attack."

A quick glance showed that their foes had summoned shields to protect them from the blaze, so an easy end to the situation was clearly not an option. He conjured a force wall to block the duo that raced forward from the street in front of the bar, mentally attached it to the buildings on either side of the alley, and extended it as high as he could without using too much power. They immediately began to batter it with their own magic, and he gasped at the intensity of the attack. "They have skills."

The flame dropped and his old friend ran past toward the three nearest them. "Yeah, I see that."

Tanyith ducked and rolled as one of the trio fired a shadow blast at his head and came up in a run toward the

Atlantean. Ahead, Dray had angled toward the other two and used two small force shields, one on each hand, to deflect the shadow magic they discharged at him. His skills were impressive and again, he was forced to acknowledge that the man in front of him was not quite the person he remembered.

In the instant before he had to focus on his own problems, his companion performed a nifty spin kick that caught the center opponent in the stomach and propelled him back. That was all the time he had to watch his friend before he was forced to block another shadow bolt with his own small shield as he closed and dispatched a kick at the other man's groin. He intercepted it with both hands, which left his face open, and Tanyith snapped his head forward and drove his forehead into his opponent's nose. It gave with a satisfying crunch and the one-two punch combination that followed felled the man, who lay moaning.

He turned to assist Dray, but his help was unnecessary. His ally pounded the man's face into the brick wall of the building opposite and dropped an elbow on the back of his neck. The Atlantean gangster fell like a stringless marionette.

His magic surged and flowed out of him with a suddenness that made his knees wobble. Four men now battered his barrier with their power and the sustained attack drained his ability to maintain it much more rapidly than the two before had. He exchanged looks with Dray, who seemed to understand the situation without words. The other man said, "Can you hold it for thirty seconds?"

"Twenty. Maybe."

He nodded. "Let's run."

They sprinted toward the other end of the alley. Three-quarters down, four more Atlanteans appeared to block their path. They skidded to a halt, and Dray laughed. "Sometimes, the only way to go…"

Tanyith remembered the phrase from similar situations years before and finished it. "Is up." He let the shield fall and blasted the ground with force magic to thrust himself upward, slightly below and to the right of his old friend.

———

Their enemies had followed quickly and after a short pursuit, they'd dodged around an obstruction and discovered a place to hide. They wriggled hastily under a huge piece of machinery while the stones and debris beneath ground into their stomachs and the metal above pressed ominously on their backs. Tanyith concealed their position while Dray cast an illusion of them running, and the Atlanteans raced after the decoy. He managed to get a closer look as they went past and saw the small earpieces they all wore, doubtless how they coordinated their activities.

He heaved a sigh of relief when a minute had passed without their return. Five minutes later, they finally dared to leave the cover of the HVAC equipment and survey their surroundings. Everything seemed safe but then again, so had the inside of the bar.

Dray asked, "What did you do to tick them off?"

He laughed. "Me? What did you do?"

The other man shrugged. "Honestly, it could be

anything. They might have been after either of us since you've made enemies among them from what I hear." Tanyith nodded. "Or maybe I ticked someone off. Like I said, we try to keep our activities on the fringes, but every now and then, there's an opportunity that's too good to pass up."

They walked along the rooftops to the end of the long block and found a fire escape to take to the ground. He was familiar with the area from his surveillance of former gang members over the last couple of weeks and led the way to a coffee shop that was open twenty-four hours and frequented by uniformed police. "You're not on the PD's radar, right?"

Dray shook his head. "Nope. I haven't been picked up in ages, and this ID is completely clean. Our people claim they've hacked the databases, too, but there hasn't been a reason to put it to the test."

He held the door for the other man and followed him in. "You have computer people? What kind of gang are you in, anyway?"

His companion laughed. "So much has changed in the last couple of years. We're almost a business, the way we operate. Specialization is the order of the day with many separate areas. And computers are a great tool to make and move money." He kept his voice low to avoid notice from the other people around, which included two patrol officers. "It's basically a requirement."

"How do you get them?"

He shrugged. "It's mostly those paying their way through college. They're smart kids who needed a break, and we keep them doing mostly above-board stuff—or at least completely deniable stuff. We have the angles covered to protect them."

They both ordered black chicory coffee and found a seat. Dray nodded. "So, you handled yourself well back there. Clearly, your instincts haven't failed you."

Tanyith laughed. "True that. Although I've used those skills a fair amount lately, so any rust was effectively scraped off before tonight."

His companion looked nervous for the first time since he had seen him after his time away. He waited in silence for him to speak, and the moment stretched uncomfortably before the man across from him sighed.

"Okay, look, here's the deal. The whole joining the gang thing is a one-time offer. Either you're in now, or you're out. I think you'd fit well with us. We wouldn't do anything that would make you uncomfortable. There are no killings and no beat-downs, except on the Atlanteans. Even then, it's almost always warning-level stuff. We know that if they turned their attention to us, they'd squash us."

Tanyith nodded. "That's a good philosophy."

"Plus, for me, it'd be nice to have someone else around who knows what the old days were like in the gang. It would add perspective on the new ways things are done. I always hope we can talk some of the Atlanteans' newbies into leaving, rather than having to damage them. You could help with that."

He nodded again. "True. I could."

"And, finally, to refuse is to formally set yourself against us. Okay, I won't personally do anything about it, but the rest of the gang will not be…uh, let's say 'well-disposed' toward you."

The laugh bubbled out unexpectedly, and he had a moment of realization about how good and how right this conversation felt. He couldn't deny that he'd often felt alone since his return to town with all his old connections gone. While he had new ones who helped to fill the gap, it wasn't the same as the depth of shared experience and time together he had with Dray. It would feel really good to have a family again the way he had before things had gone wrong.

But it won't be like that, no matter how much I want it to be. Dray will be cool, but the others definitely won't. They'll know I'm not the same as them. He shook his head. *Besides, it's time to look forward. Cali, Zeb, and even Barton—they're my people now.*

Dray took the motion as an answer, which it essentially was although he hadn't intended it as such. He rose and extended a hand. "I get it. Totally. Like I said, you and me, we're good. If you need me, you know where to find me."

He stood and grasped it firmly. "Same thing the other way, Dray."

They released simultaneously, and his friend walked out the door. Tanyith sat in his chair and sipped his coffee, filled with both loss and relief. With a sigh, he shook his head again. He muttered, "Way to go, Tay. You managed to push away your only remaining friend from the old days and lose a source of information to help find your damn target."

Twenty minutes later, the coffee consumed, he wandered into the night feeling untethered and alone but somehow sure he'd made the right decision. *Sometimes, the only way to go is up.*

CHAPTER FOURTEEN

The New Orleans Public Library was one of Cali's favorite places to do schoolwork—or at least it had been before her life had become so crazy busy with people kidnapping her, manipulating her, and trying to kill her. Her smile grew with each approaching step when she saw the whirls and colored markings that made up the mural on the side of the white building. She'd spent many an hour inside its cool chambers, working or simply pretending to in order to have an air-conditioned retreat from the blazing sun.

She strode along the sidewalk beside it, looked through the windows, and saw any number of people making use of the space. Some worked at computers, some browsed, and at least a couple used the opportunity to indulge in a short nap. She was always most amused when local business people in suits and ties and with obvious hangovers spent their lunch breaks sleeping in the building's relative privacy. The librarians were amenable to a point but snoring or taking up space someone else needed to use would get one thrown out with no remorse.

Within moments, she climbed the short stairs at the front and entered the huge structure. Three-quarters of the building had a two-story-high ceiling, while the remainder was a single story under a second floor. Glass surrounded it all so the sun provided the main illumination, complemented by fluorescent fixtures high above. Rows of bookshelves extended from the front to the back, each with the appropriate alphabetic or Dewey decimal index on the ends, a scattering of round tables, and a section on the side with computers for public use.

Caliste had never visited the part of the library she was headed to now, though. While she'd noticed gnome librarians several times, she'd simply appreciated the lack of discrimination shown by whoever ran the place, completely unaware that a second library existed beneath the one she knew so well. Apparently, a long time before, the gnomes had excavated and magically protected the area beneath the structure and slowly expanded it until it was ready for occupation. Then, they'd secured copies of the most important magical texts and organized them into the city's premier location for magical research. One could find information on the Internet and any number of shops in the Quarter claimed to sell magical tomes, but from what she'd heard, the gnomish library was the real deal.

Excitement stirred as she followed the instructions she'd been provided with and walked through the entire first floor to the very back corner of the room, where a paneled door with a brass knob marked *Staff Only* stood closed and looked decidedly forbidding. She tried the handle and it failed to turn as she'd known it would. *Still, I had to check, right?* She whispered an incantation and placed her hand flat on the panel as she'd been instructed, then pushed force magic into it. The door swung open without protest, and she darted through quickly and closed it softly behind her. A short staircase illuminated by only a single bulb took her to another door, and she repeated the process.

When she emerged into the magical library, having no idea what to expect, her jaw dropped in awe. She was on the third level of a three-story structure, a long rectangle that stretched ahead of her to end a hundred feet or more in the distance. Overhead, an arched ceiling covered the space in a soft blue-tinted glow. No lights were visible, so she presumed it must be magic. *It certainly looks magical—all of it.* The staircase in front of her was made of etched glass, as were the sides and stairs. She walked down them carefully and stared at the symbols and pictures carved into the thick panes, unable to distinguish any apparent order to them. The first displayed the solar system, the next looked like Arabic writing, and the one after that showed a math equation she couldn't even begin to understand.

The staircase ended at the second level, which extended over the center of the space and covered the middle third through most of the length. It had a parquet floor with a design that reminded her of the Q-bert game Dasante had made her play on a toy he'd bought. A bright red leather couch stood across from a wooden coffee table and two upholstered chairs, also in scarlet. Stairs led down to the left and right beyond them, and farther along the second level were three desks arranged in a U shape and covered with books and papers as if someone had stepped away for a moment.

She walked carefully between the beautiful furniture and stretched a hand out to touch an illuminated manuscript on the coffee table, feeling a slight tingle of arcane power from the contact. *Holy hell, this is amazing. How did I not know this was here?* Even from inside, truly believing that she was under the library was a difficult idea to accept. She noticed belatedly that the walls to either side, all three stories high, were fashioned from bookshelves and filled with exquisite objects. These were mostly books, naturally, but also statues and wands on display and other items of magic she didn't recognize the function of at all.

In absolute awe, she stepped carefully to the bottom floor and again reviewed the images on each pane of glass she transited. The ground level was filled with standing desks, each containing more books and some with large maps and unbound sheets of what looked like vellum. She shook her head, amazed by the grandeur of the space—and the fact that it was underground and probably underwater, to boot. It felt like neither of those things and rather like a refuge among the clouds.

Okay. I'm in love.

Several people were present on the bottom level. A wizard stood at a desk and paged through a book with waves of his wand. A Drow female with short white hair in a very trendy style browsed a bookcase. At the back of the room and behind an intricately carved table covered in logbooks sat the person she was looking for. She approached quickly, her quiet boots soft on the wooden floor, and slipped into the chair opposite him. Unwilling to break the stillness of the incredible place, she simply waited patiently to be noticed.

After several moments, he slid a bookmark into the open page and closed the book gently. He smiled at her over his perfectly braided white beard and the mustache above his upper lip stretched wide. "Caliste. It's so nice to finally see you in person."

"Cali, please," she replied. "You're exactly as Zeb described you. Especially the beard. It is my honor to meet you, Scoppic." He beamed at her. Her boss had told her that showing respect was essential as gnomes tended to inhabit the more formal end of the social expectations spectrum. And, in truth, anyone who worked in this place and had a hand in creating it deserved every amount of respect she could convey. "This is amazing. Beyond words. Well, beyond my words."

He laughed. "Mine as well. But you are here for a purpose, I believe. How may I help you?"

She nodded and pulled her phone out. "I'm looking for information on two things. First, the sword that this is a piece of." She called the image up and showed it to him, holding the device over the desk. He leaned forward and stared at it for almost a full minute without speaking, then returned to his former position.

"It is almost certainly Atlantean. Those are very old Atlantean glyphs from a version of the language that predates the current one. I can point you in the right direction for some research on that topic."

Her heart beat extra rapidly at the revelation that there might be a light at the end of her tunnel. "The next challenge is a little harder, I think." She swiped through a few images, then turned the phone toward him again. "This is a book my parents left for me. It's either in a code or in a language I don't understand. Do you know anything about it?"

He responded more quickly this time. "No. I believe your first supposition is correct—that it is a code—as it looks like no tongue I have ever seen. While we do have excellent books on code-breaking, I don't think that's quite what you were looking for."

On another day, his response might have disappointed her. Today, though, in this grand place and with the answer to one of her questions potentially nearby, she was willing to let that slide. "No problem. How about you point me to the books about swords?"

It wasn't quite that easy, naturally. For those skilled in telekinesis, accessing materials would probably be a breeze. In her case, Scoppic had to escort her to the appropriate bookshelf and summon the correct tomes to float to the couch she had claimed. He had recommended six, the smallest as thick as her clenched fist and the largest about twice that size. She wanted to ask him for guidance but had the feeling it would make her look stupid, which she definitely didn't want. Not in this place.

Instead, she simply chose the first and opened it. The heavy leather cover was soft on her palms and the inside pages elegantly handwritten. It was like holding history in her hands. *Okay, focus. You're here for a reason other than to indulge your love of books.* With a mental promise to return sometime simply for pleasure, she flicked carefully through the leaves of paper and scanned for headings or pictures that referenced swords. The tome was on the topic of artifacts in general, and although she found mentions of the weapons in several places, it was a broad discussion.

The next one was about Atlantean weapons and mentioned swords often but not artifacts at all. She made a mental note to come back to it in her next visit as a picture of a warrior fighting with a trident and a net seemed like it might one day be relevant. The third book was entirely about Rhazdon artifacts. She'd heard of the half-Atlantean who had wreaked havoc on Oriceran but knew little about him—or was it her? *I'll ask Emalia when I have the chance. It could have a bearing on this, I suppose.*

In the fourth book, she hit pay dirt. The text discussed the history of Atlantis and a set of swords figured prominently. They were elegant weapons, the hilts long enough to accommodate a double-handed grip and the blades a shining silver-white with runes etched across every inch. Only the pommels differed, each decorated with a different kind of gem. There were nine swords, each associated with a family name that sounded old and august.

She turned the page to find a description of each of the weapons. As she read it, a chill swept over her. Emalia had been correct on several counts. Each sword was different and concurred with her great aunt's knowledge of the artifacts and went far beyond in reputed abilities. Because the actual blades and their engravings were identical, it was impossible to know which one her parents had left her a piece of or if the other shard she'd seen was truly part of the same weapon. *But it has to be. There are no coincidences that big.*

Cali shut the tome and set it aside before she took a long, calming breath. A quick perusal of the remaining tomes added nothing. She let the tumult in her mind run free and focused her mind to simply look around the space, admire it, and bathe in the serenity of it. When she felt she could maintain her calm, she took the books to the gnome's desk.

He looked up from his records with a smile. "Did you find what you were looking for?"

"Oh yes. Could you keep this handy for me? I'll ask my great aunt to come take a peek later today."

He reached out and accepted the book that had provided the most information. "Of course. I look forward to seeing her."

Cali set the remainder in a stack on a corner of his desk, not knowing what to do with them, and forced a smile. "Thank you so much for your help. Truly, this is a magnificent place."

Scoppic nodded with a broad grin. "You are welcome anytime."

"Oh, I'll be back." *As soon as I get over the fact that my parents somehow came into possession of one of the magical swords that had been given only to the ruling families of Atlantis.*

CHAPTER FIFTEEN

Tanyith crept carefully through the sunset shadows around the back of the house and kept his head low so it wouldn't be visible to anyone inside. The precaution was probably unnecessary as he'd cloaked himself in an illusion that would allow him to blend into the natural dark areas, but it never hurt to be careful. A few days before, he'd tracked his current target, Gina Johnson, to this location. Since then, he had been unable to reacquire her. She worked for a bank but had been absent for two days. Her mother lived across town but hours spent watching that location hadn't turned anything up either.

His instincts told him it couldn't be a coincidence. There was absolutely no way that someone he was tracking would vanish unless it was related to his search. And even if a small possibility that it was random chance existed, that didn't change the need to find out what was going on. He peeked around the rear right corner of the house, hoping he'd see her on the porch with a drink and a friend, but found only empty silence.

He defeated the back door easily with his lock pick gun and stepped into the small kitchen it opened into. The home was trapped in the seventies with orange countertops and an old ivory refrigerator, a yellow stove and oven, and no dishwasher but rather a drying rack with a few dishes and a bowl resting in it. He traced his fingers across them and confirmed that they were dry. A whispered word changed his cloaking spell to one that would work indoors where shadows weren't plentiful, albeit less well. He'd never managed sufficient skill to totally do away with the strange visible ripple that sometimes appeared. Still, once again, it never hurt to be careful.

The room had two exits, one to a hallway and the other to a dining room. He took the latter and squeezed his way around the large table and chairs that filled most of the space. The furniture looked older than the house and would require a team of people to move it in or out.

Gina had left the gang voluntarily—before his own involuntary departure—to move in with someone she'd dated for a year. Everyone had wished her well, and he imagined she'd fallen off the gang's radar shortly thereafter. Yet the house where she now lived was that of a single person and felt empty. He maneuvered through the small living room and checked the front door. It was locked with the chain in place. *It's not that weird. Many people use their back doors instead of the front when they head out to work.* The logic failed to overcome the rapidly growing sense of concern that had brought him to the house.

Tanyith walked quietly up the stairs and kept his weight on his back leg as he tested each new step for creaks. He avoided the center portion and positioned his feet near the wall and the railing. A small bathroom came into view as he climbed and again reminded him of something from several decades before. He shook his head as thoughts tumbled through it. *What happened to the guy? Is this the house she moved into then or another one she moved into after? And, most importantly, where the hell is she?*

A linen closet revealed nothing interesting, so he turned his attention to the two doorways on the hall leading toward the front of the house. He approached cautiously and looked around the corner of the first. It was the size of a small bedroom and served mainly as a closet but held a narrow computer desk with disconnected cables resting on the top, presumably for a laptop. He took a step inside and examined her clothes and had to grin at the collection of jeans and hoodies that took up one side. *You can take a person out of the gang, but you can't take the gang out of the person.* If he hadn't been sent to prison, he was sure his wardrobe would include similar items.

He reversed the step that had brought him into the room and moved down the hall to repeat the process. When he found nothing awaiting him, he entered her bedroom. It was half again as large as the last room and held a queen-size bed, a dresser, and a vanity table. A stack of translucent bins held makeup and other personal care products when he pulled them open. A search of the dresser and the vanity was as fruitless as the rest of his efforts had been. He was about to start to take things apart in either good investigative tactics or frustration when a strange sound froze him in his tracks.

Tense and alert, he waited, listening, and heard a

creaking that seemed to emanate from above. Following the noise, he paced into the office-slash-closet and examined the ceiling. Above the clothes was the outline of a square. *An attic. Okay.* The general heat in New Orleans meant most people didn't use the highest parts of the house, if they even had them, for anything other than storage, so checking up there hadn't occurred to him. He dragged the chair over and pushed up on the cutout area. It gave easily and he tossed the drywall section off to the side.

Muttering curses under his breath for the stupid thing he was about to do, he jumped, grasped the edges of the attic floor, and pulled himself through the opening. Tanyith crouched above it, his hands raised defensively with shields of shimmering force held in each, but no attack came. He maintained that position while his heartbeat returned to a normal rate, then dispelled one of them. Quickly, he cast a simple light charm—basically lightning magic bound into a small sphere—and rolled it along the floor away from him. It took two more before most of the room was no longer in darkness.

It was a storage space of plywood over rafters with dusty pink insulation visible at the edges. In the center of the room lay a prone figure with its back to him, and the dull silver of duct tape covered its wrists and hands. The black hair that spread around the head gave him mixed hope and fear that he'd found Gina. He stepped forward, knowing a minute either way wouldn't make a difference and wary of a trap. Nothing materialized, and he circled the body.

Blood stained the floor in front of her face, which had seeped there from her skull. She was too pale, but relief flooded him when her chest moved. He touched her cheek and whispered, "Gina. Can you hear me?" She didn't respond, and he weighed the choices of moving her or calling for help. The head wound made his decision for him. He pulled his cell phone out and called for an ambulance. There would be ways to connect with her later—at the hospital maybe—once she was taken care of.

He couldn't stay for the police and couldn't give her the reassurance of sharing the ambulance ride with her, but at the very least he could unbind her hands. He retrieved his pocketknife, sawed at the duct tape, and pulled her arms free when it parted.

Later, he wouldn't be sure whether he heard it or saw it first. The device was small but its shape was unmistakable. Instinct propelled him and he threw his body on top of Gina's and summoned a force shield around them both.

The grenade was an incendiary. The initial explosion sent flame in all directions, but none of it penetrated his defenses. He had time to think. *Okay, I can wait until the nearest flames die out and then get us out of here by blasting a hole in the roof.* Unfortunately, the rest of the trap activated. The sparks triggered a series of other explosives that had been planted all through the rafters. He held her tightly as the force blew the top of the house off and they careened helplessly, driven by the force of the blast.

If they hadn't been shielded, the grenade would have at least hurt him and probably killed Gina. The explosion would have ensured their deaths and destroyed most of the evidence as well. As it was, he struggled to maintain the shield as they plummeted and wrenched his body around so he wouldn't land on her. Flaming debris battered them on the way down, and he tried frantically to calculate the right moment to act. Finally, with the ground no more than eight feet below them, he banished the shield and summoned his force magic to control their fall. He managed to successfully bleed off the speed so that when they landed, it was as if they'd fallen only a reasonable distance instead of from the top of a building.

It was enough to drive the air from his lungs and leave him reeling in pain from the impact of his body with the ground and the woman's with his. He finally managed to gasp in some oxygen and rolled her carefully off him onto the grass. *She's still breathing, good. Hang in there, Gina.* He heard shouts and the screeching of tires and forced himself into motion. *I can't be caught. They'll ask too many questions.* He stumbled toward her back yard and summoned a portal as soon as he reached the darkness, plunged through it, and closed it immediately.

Tanyith thumped painfully on the carpeted floor of his living room. The small apartment was bare and a mattress in the bedroom was his only furniture at the moment. He crawled to a wall and used it as a support to push to his feet, then staggered into the bathroom. In the medicine cabinet was the red vial he sought and would have carried with him if he hadn't been overconfident and stupid. He drained it, dropped the container, and managed to get under the covers before the exhaustion of the event rendered him unable to move any longer.

Questions kept him from falling asleep, however. The ones he'd had all along were still there and still bothered him. Where had Sienna's ex-boyfriend Aiden Walsh, aka Adam Harlan, aka Harry disappeared to? What made him so difficult to track? How were the Atlanteans involved, and how was Dray's group involved? Now, however, there was a new and far more worrisome factor to consider.

How did they know I was looking for Gina, and why do they want to stop me from finding Aiden? And who are "they," anyway? No answers surfaced before he finally succumbed to slumber.

CHAPTER SIXTEEN

Her alarm hadn't managed to wake her that morning
because Tanyith had texted her with details of his
adventures from the night before. Cali wasn't able to get
back to sleep thereafter, so she'd spent the time straighten-
ing her apartment, grateful to have so much space even
though it required more upkeep than her last home.

The class at the dojo had been good, and her personal
session with Ikehara better. He'd asked her to come in the
next day, which was a rare closed Sunday for the martial
arts studio, to do extra cleaning. She didn't consider refus-
ing. A serious amount of pride came with being within her
teacher's trusted inner circle, and that would have been
enough to motivate her even without the additional
training he'd provided.

She'd run home afterward and enjoyed the exercise. All
the damage from the battle with the Atlanteans had faded,
and it was good to feel completely confident in her body
again. *When I see Nylotte, I need to ask her what the deal is with
the healing potion not working like it should.* Zeb hadn't

known the answer and the Drow was her second-best option.

A half-hour under the hot water was a glorious end to the first part of the day, and she took a few extra minutes to get her hair under control, putting moisturizing product in it and brushing it through. She still had four hours before she had to be at the tavern and had arranged with Dasante to spend that time busking in Jackson Square.

Once she'd pulled on shorts, sneakers, and a t-shirt, she called, "Up and at 'em, Fyre." The Draksa gave something between a yawn and a growl from the front room, and she laughed as she entered and found him stretching like a cat with his rear end sticking up. "Honestly, you are the strangest creature." He opened his mouth and lolled his tongue at her but didn't respond.

Cali rolled her eyes. "Put your costume on, doofus." The air rippled as he changed, but she continued to see the Draksa where anyone else would see a Rottweiler of one shade or another. She'd realized he varied his color from comments that others who saw him had made. With a shake of her head, she walked into the hallway and took a few steps to Dasante's door.

A post-it note was attached to it. *Got tired of waiting. See you over there.*

She looked at Fyre with a grin. "Why must you make us late for everything?"

"Yes, it's me that's the problem," he drawled.

"You know it, scaly." She led him down the stairs and out the door, and they shared a happy walk toward the heart of the French Quarter. Along the way, they encountered the usual things—restaurant windows framing tourists having lunch, frozen drink bars serving the early afternoon crowd that wanted to get a jump on their party, and artists plying their trades for tips wherever they could find a space. While the Square was her favorite place, some found it too busy and didn't enjoy the competition. Maybe, if it was her primary source of income, she'd feel the same. She said a small word of thanks to the universe for the relative stability she had compared to others she met on the streets.

They arrived and Fyre dashed ahead to greet Dasante, acting like a dog happy to see his owner. Her friend laughed, and she shook her head as she bumped the Draksa out of the way and exchanged their secret handshake and a fist bump with her neighbor. "What's shaking, D?"

He shrugged. "I've been doing basic stuff. Clean comedy. Warming up the brain. Not that you'd know anything about that."

Cali chuckled sarcastically. "Yeah, yeah, I'm well aware of your brain and the limited possibilities thereof. What are you thinking for today? Magic show?" She'd noticed the suitcase that expanded into a performance table and contained his implements and collapsible top hat.

"Probably. But I wondered... Can you, like, read minds now?"

"No. I can't and wouldn't unless it was essential, even if I could. Why?"

"I was trying to come up with a new act. Doing a matchmaker gig to find out who might be compatible with each other, that kind of deal. But if you can't read minds, it won't work."

She thought about what she'd learned recently. Her

telepathy was fairly good, as was her direct mental magic. She hadn't practiced the indirect distraction in a while but was sure it would come when she needed it. Force magic and unpredictable fire rounded her skills out. "No, I can't. But I do still have my ability to detect someone's intentions by touching them." Dasante and Emalia were the only ones who knew about that one. "Could we put that to some use?"

He pulled an oversized coin from his pocket and made it appear and disappear repeatedly as he considered it. "We might be able to play it off like you're an extension of my magical ability if you touched them and sent me a thought about what you got from them. It seems a little convoluted, though."

"Agreed. Plus, I'd have to touch all those strangers. Ew." They laughed together.

"Okay," he said finally. "Dasante the amazing and magnificent magician it is. Give me a few minutes to get set up." She snatched one of the balls from his kit and went to play with Fyre inside the fenced area of the grounds. The Draksa complained from time to time about being forced to behave like a dog while playing fetch, but she was sure it was merely blather and that he actually enjoyed it. Either way, it was something they could do together without attracting notice.

After a few throws, they wound up seated next to each other on the ground. D was still a few minutes away from being ready. She focused her magic and looked around. It was no longer necessary to picture an actual mind or balloon to manage telepathy. That part had become automatic. Cali was able to easily transmit a message to anyone she could see unless they were actively blocking, something that magicals apparently could do. Emalia had told her some of her upcoming training would need to be focused on managing her own internal barriers, which opened whenever she performed mental magic.

She willed words into Fyre's mind. "It's a beautiful day to not have anyone trying to kill us, don't you think?"

He snorted in response and through the hand resting on his back, she tasted the pineapple cinnamon mix that usually accompanied humor, a mixture of mischief, and positive feelings toward her. At one time, she'd thought that the ability to sense others' moods or intentions would be the strongest magic she possessed. Now, it merely felt like a manual tool in an ever-expanding box of powered equipment.

Of course, where the Draksa was concerned, she usually knew what he was feeling from his expressions. Each day brought them closer together, and she wondered where that would end. Already, she couldn't imagine a life without him. He barked suddenly and dashed away, and she laughed until it hurt when she realized that the magical dragon lizard from Atlantis was chasing two squirrels and generally losing the race.

Finally, she composed herself and called Fyre back to her as she gathered a handful of small wildflowers that grew nearby. They headed over to where Dasante had positioned his tools on his unfolded case which sat atop a shaky support, donned the long sleeve shirt with the cuffs rolled that he wore for the role, and placed the top hat in a position to accept contributions from a hopefully entertained crowd. She took her place before the table and motioned for the dragon lizard to sit behind her.

In her barker's voice, loud and eager, she yelled, "Come one, come all, to see the Amazing Dasante! His mystical arts and superior sleight-of-hand cannot fail to impress." She continued the patter as people walked past and occasionally called them by name and looked for her favorite target, a twenty-something man with a companion on his arm. She found him and shouted, "You, sir, show your lady friend a good time by exposing her to the magic of the Stupendous Dasante."

They laughed and looked embarrassed but as usual, it didn't stop them from coming over. Her partner launched into his routine, which always started with the magic rings that only he could unlock, several card tricks that relied on a marked deck and a truly skilled ability to read subtle reactions when he whipped through the possibilities for a given card, and finally, the three-card-monte inspired ball and cups trick. The man got it right, and she rewarded him with a dandelion, to everyone's amusement.

They left, and a bill fluttered into the top hat as they passed. She exchanged a grin with Dasante and yelled again. "See the mystical magician and his mighty canine companion. Dasante and Fyre, here for your delight." The laughs came from behind her this time as well, and she gave herself over to the joy of being an entertainer.

By the time she had to leave for work, she'd earned half as much as she'd make in tips that night, which would be a busy shift. She exchanged fist bumps with D and knelt to give Fyre a hug. She whispered, "Are you coming to the tavern or staying here with the magical man?" He stood and leaned against her leg to indicate the former. "Long way or shortcut?"

He trotted in the direction of the Drunken Dragons many blocks away, which was answer enough. She grinned. "You're right. It's entirely too nice not to enjoy the incredibly long walk to work, after which I'll have to be on my feet all night while you sleep behind the bar." He snorted and increased his pace. *Damn dragon.*

CHAPTER SEVENTEEN

The next morning, Cali was up and moving before her alarm. She was eager to go to the dojo and get the cleaning out of the way, with the promise of another day of lucrative busking afterward. Plus, she hoped to have time to stop and talk to Emalia since the woman flatly refused to share any non-emergency information by any means other than face to face. Her great aunt should have visited the library by now and might have more knowledge on the sword—or on the charms, which she'd taken on as her own special project.

It was a pleasure not to find a message waiting for her on the real entrance when she arrived. She'd felt comfortable enough about the reality of the promised interval that she didn't demand Fyre come with her, and to have that belief at least partially confirmed was a step in the right direction.

Cali let her mind wander as she worked and mulled over the many things going on in her life. While she used a mop to damp-wash the canvas mat, she considered the open questions that vexed her. Chief among them was the sword, of course, but she couldn't do much with that until her great aunt weighed in. She laughed internally as she realized that all the others seemed equally out of reach at the moment.

She had a key to part of an address—1601. That would be the easiest thing to make progress on next, as there couldn't be that many buildings with that address. She put it at the top of her mental agenda. After that came the book. If it was actually written in code as Scoppic had concluded and not in an existing language, she was well and truly stymied unless something unexpected transpired. *So, we'll hope for something unexpected on that one. Next.*

She swapped the damp mop for a dry one and ran it carefully over the mat. Her bare feet squished as they gripped the surface, instinctively seeking solid footing on the yielding canvas. An image of her parents as they'd been while alive and well swam into her mind without provocation. She didn't realize that tears welled in her eyes until one fell on the mat, and she dashed them away with the back of her hand. *God, I miss you guys. I hope all those people who say we'll meet again are right.*

Cali moved to the lobby and looked through the windows. The weather was a little overcast, which fit her thoughtful mood well. Her teacher's desk was clear, as always, and she dug in the cupboard at the base of a large display cabinet for the polish and wax. She sprayed it and the lemon scent wafted up and made her sneeze, then laughed at her own joke as she muttered, "Wax on, wax off." Her brain turned from questions to plans.

I need to find a third for the next battle, and I need to find the 1601 place. Everything else is in holding until other people do things. She didn't like the situation but was also keenly aware that she had too much on her plate to handle alone. Even though she'd asked Zeb to join her mostly as a joke, she wouldn't have turned him down if he'd unexpectedly accepted. Tanyith was her main prospect, however. She knew he'd be willing to do it since he'd made it clear he would have joined her for the two-on-two. *I wonder where this ends? Hundreds against hundreds?* She realized she'd missed her chance to check that while at the library and sighed. *There is too much stuff going on, for sure.*

With the desk shining, she turned her attention to the shelves of the display cabinet. She cleaned the little rectangular and square sections one by one, emptied them, polished them, then ran a different cloth over the pictures or trophies or paraphernalia that lived inside before she returned everything to its place. Every so often, she'd discover that something had changed and she hadn't noticed it, and that was the case this morning. A picture that had formerly been of Ikehara alone on a mountain hike of some kind now showed him in a similar endeavor but with two children at his sides. The sight made her smile. She knew about his family from putting together small pieces of information gathered at random, but most people probably didn't. They looked happy and so did he. She returned it to its place and moved on to the next.

Vacuuming drowned out her mental voice and for a time, only the work existed, almost a Zen experience of no-mindedness. She finished with the bathrooms and changing rooms, and four hours or so after she'd arrived, she was finally ready to head out and get on with her day.

The sense of satisfaction she always felt after working at the dojo carried her happily down the street for a block, and one of the poppy playlists Dasante had created for her beat in her earbuds and put a bounce in her step.

The good vibes came to an abrupt end as the magical radar she'd sent out with no results for weeks suddenly pinged a warning. Cali forced herself not to change her movements and to bop along in time to the music, but her senses focused as she tried to identify what had tripped her internal alarm system. She had a sense of distance and of hostile intention but not dire threat, although she couldn't be sure whether those intuitions were accurate. The talent was new, lightly trained, and difficult to interpret. *It's off to the right, whatever it is.* She added a head twist to her walking dance and looked in both directions. It took another thirty seconds before she saw what had triggered her danger sense.

The woman moved like an athlete and the running shorts and loose t-shirt she wore emphasized that image. Long, darkish hair was bound in a ponytail and a phone was strapped to her bicep. She jogged slowly, at about the same pace as Cali's fast walk, which was doubtless one of the indicators that had attracted her notice. A black strap was visible around her waist, probably for a small bag.

Now that she'd identified the potential threat, she kept moving. The person was a block away and she'd have sufficient time to react if that changed. She pushed more power into her magical sense and tried to both make it more focused on the areas closest to her and also push the boundaries out further. It required her to segment her mind and dedicate a part to each task, which was difficult to do without changing her behavior. Her ongoing practice in mental magic paid off, though, and she detected the hint of a threat from her left, more or less where she'd expected it might be. *None of our enemies so far have been foolish enough to come alone. I can't see why that would change.*

The man on the opposite side looked like a business type in a blue Oxford shirt with the collar undone and khaki pants. Like the woman, he kept pace with her and studiously didn't look at her. *Okay, there are two, at least. I think I can safely assume they are probably not Atlanteans since they don't wear the uniform and that gang is supposed to leave me alone.* She turned right at the next block to test them.

Sure enough, after she took another left to head in the proper direction, they were in place again after a couple of blocks. While it would be fairly easy to escape, she was curious about who they were and what they were up to, so she decided to turn the tables. *But let's not be stupid about it.* She pictured her scaly life-partner in her mind and sent a thought to him. Practice had allowed her to keep the connection open once she'd initiated it, and although he couldn't send worded messages, the wash of approval she received was a clear answer. She calculated it would take him five minutes or so to be in the air over her position and began to look for a place to make her play.

The sight of the St Louis Cathedral spires over the rooftops ahead felt like fate. It was Sunday, so it would be open for services. If she recalled the times correctly, she'd arrive shortly after the last one. The church would remain accessible for the entire day, though, so she'd be able to duck inside with ease. Cali sent a mental message explaining the plan to Fyre and again received approval in return. She wasn't sure if he would get inside before her or simply wait as backup, but either option worked for her. If she had to choose, the sight of him in the sanctuary would be something definitely worth seeing.

She approached the beautiful cathedral from behind and once again truly bopped along to the music in her ears, confident in what was about to play out. After a left turn into the square, she strode up the stairs of the church, stepped inside, and quick-walked forward down the center aisle. It was a grand space with an arched ceiling high above decorated with gorgeous murals and filigree. The majority of the surfaces were white but every other color could be found in the paintings and ornamentation. The altar at the far end shined with gold. The floor was made of black and white marble squares set in diamond shapes, and dark wooden pews ran on her left and right down the length of the immense space.

Halfway down, she stopped and slid into an unoccupied row, ducked down momentarily, and cast a simple veil to hide herself before she straightened. Since her magic had been fully released, her ability to become invisible when motionless had improved dramatically. She still wasn't totally skilled at moving in secret, but Emalia assured her it would come with time. *And practice, of course. Always with practice.*

Another whispered spell created an illusion of her seated several rows ahead, again not near anyone else. She turned her head slowly toward the rear of the sanctuary. *Now to wait for developments to, uh...develop.* The delay wasn't long. The man entered first, moved nonchalantly down the center aisle, and seemed immune to the grandeur around him. He looked ordinary, seemed to fit in with the others in the sparse crowd, and his lips twitched slightly as he noticed the back of her illusion's head. He moved to his left, sat in a pew, and adopted a position with his gaze lowered that was doubtless supposed to look like prayer.

Cali had almost convinced herself to blast him with a force bolt when she realized that her anger level had risen while she stared at him. Only the arrival of an old woman who made her way carefully down the center aisle jarred her from the internal discussion she hadn't even known she'd had. *What the hell?* She shook her head. *Focus, Cali.*

Behind the older woman came the younger one who'd followed her. She stopped near the back and took a seat on the same side of the church as her. Cali's eyes narrowed as the implications banged around her brain. *They must be communicating somehow. I guess it's possible I didn't hear him and they're using radios. Or they could be magicals. Is there another magical group in town getting ready to cause trouble? If so, why are they looking at me?* The former proposition seemed much more likely than the latter, but she couldn't be sure. She needed more information. Fortunately, that was part of the plan.

She sent a telepathic message to Fyre. *Distraction, please.* A few moments later, a loud bang emanated from the rear of the sanctuary that sounded like one of the entry doors slammed shut. It was followed an instant later by the same sound again. Everyone twisted toward the noise except her, and she vanished the illusory version of herself. When the man turned again, his alarm was clear as he suddenly stood and moved toward the front of the cathedral, looking in every direction to see where she'd disappeared to.

Very slowly, she turned her invisible head so it would stay unseen and saw the woman exit the building, followed moments later by her cohort. When they had both gone, she rose and walked out behind them at a safe distance. There was no risk of losing them with the veiled Draksa on the case. She could always sense his presence with minimal effort and easily followed Fyre while he followed the woman. Occasionally, she caught sight of her in the distance. Her gaze was on them when the man joined her and they had an intense discussion that involved arm waving and voices almost loud enough to hear before they turned to walk together toward the edge of the Quarter.

Cali continued to trail them, but when they got into a car, her part of the surveillance was over. She told Fyre to stay on the duo and found a secluded place to portal from. Her head was in her books when he returned an hour later, flew through the window she'd left open for that purpose, and landed gracefully in the open space near the front door. She greeted him with a grin. "Hey, it's about time you got back."

He snorted and shook his head. "It's lucky you have someone with actual skills in surveillance to rely on."

She shrugged. "We can't all be invisible birds, you know." The provocation drew the growl she wanted, and she laughed. "I'm kidding. You're amazing and I am lucky to know you. So, what did you find out?"

He lowered himself to a seated position and raised his head but didn't speak.

"Okay, I'm sorry I called you a bird." She sighed. "Are you happy now?"

"Hardly, but it will do for the moment. Your two admirers went to a restaurant. They were only inside for a few minutes, but I hung around for a while longer to see what would happen. One of the men who were with the Zatora leader came out a while later."

"That fits. It makes sense they'd keep an eye on me, I guess. Why not? Apparently, everyone else does. But at least it's not a new magical gang in town. That would suck. We have more than enough problems with the one we already have." She checked her watch and stood with a groan. "Okay. Nap, shower, then work. Our window for investigation today is at an end. But let's think about how we can quit being the watched and become the watchers." *It's time to flip the script on these jerks.*

CHAPTER EIGHTEEN

I t was never really much of a surprise when Detective Kendra Barton arrived at the Drunken Dragons Tavern. Whether she was there to chat with Zeb—who appeared to have become her go-between with the magical community—with Tanyith, who she clearly had the hots for, or simply to harass her, she seemed to appear fairly regularly. For her to arrive so close to closing, though, wasn't normal at all. *Unless she hoped Tay would be here for a booty call or something. Ew.* She was in the same coat she'd worn the first time Cali had seen her—the shiny brown number—which meant she'd probably come from work. The light professional makeup increased that probability.

She watched out of the corner of her eye as the woman took the seat at the very end of the bar farthest from the door. That was notable because people normally chose the same places and she couldn't recall the detective selecting that one before. Of course, it was possible she had done it on one of her few nights off, but it still struck her as weird.

Also weird was the way she leaned forward to talk to

Zeb. Cali had become a fairly good interpreter of body language, and hers definitely showed at least nervousness or agitation, maybe more. She angled toward the conversation, deposited empties beside the representative from the NOPD, and shouted drink orders at her boss before she turned to the other woman with a smirk. "Don't let me interrupt your leisure with my working, Detective."

She received a thin smile in response but nothing more. *That's also notable and also alarming.* Barton allowing a chance to insult her to pass without taking advantage of it was virtually unprecedented. Maybe it had happened at the docks, but otherwise, she was always ready with one thing or another.

Zeb interjected, "Here are your drinks. Go, and take final orders. We'll close on time tonight." He, too, seemed less happy than usual. *What the hell is going on here?* She circulated through the crowd and reminded them the clock was ticking. Her next hour was a haze of work and convincing people it was time to go, which culminated in her having to physically push the last patrons out the door. She didn't generally mind since it was all part of the game, but she was thankful it wasn't a Kilomea today. The giant beings saw everything physical as a contest, and it was a true chore getting them to leave. Finally, though, the room was empty except for the three of them and Fyre, who dozed in his usual place.

Cali took the seat next to the detective with a sigh. "What, she doesn't have to follow the rules? Seriously, Zeb, I'm starting to doubt your judgment."

He shook his head, an obvious refusal to engage in the banter. *What is with people today?* "You'll feel differently when you hear what she has to say." *Well, that doesn't sound good.*

She turned to Barton. "Let's have it."

The detective skipped that opportunity for a sarcastic comeback too. "There's been disturbing chatter from informants we have around the Atlanteans."

"How is that different than usual? Those idiots always cause trouble."

The woman shook her head and her short black hair flipped into her face. She summoned an annoyed look. "Yeah, this is something else. If you'll shut up for a minute, I can explain."

That's more like it. She grinned. "Please avail me of your knowledge, oh wise one."

With an exasperated sigh, the detective finished the amber liquid in the pint glass before her and handed it to Zeb. He pulled a draft handle, a low ABV Oktoberfest that was still hanging around, and returned it to her. "Okay, here's the deal. We've always had people watching the Atlantean gang, cultivating contacts inside it, that kind of thing. Since we're a multi-bureau initiative, we also have access to the feds' info too, although it constantly comes down the chain late and highly sanitized." She laughed. "They have trust issues."

Cali echoed her amusement. "Don't we all." Zeb nodded from his position on a high stool behind the bar. His arms were folded and his eyes were intense, both deviations from his normal affable bartender pose.

Barton continued. "Anyway, we've received really strange information from them. We anticipated hearing a considerable amount about the drugs they've pushed, but it seems they're much more committed to them than expected. Basically, the gang has rolled back all the other stuff they were doing to blanket the streets with their new product. It has the narcotics folks concerned."

She frowned. "It doesn't sound like them. They've always been kind of diversified, right? Tanyith gave me that impression, anyway."

The detective nodded. "Exactly. The Atlanteans have been slow and steady all along, expanding their sphere of influence without upsetting any apple carts. And now, they're pushing hard."

"So, what caused the change?" Zeb asked. "Do you have any ideas?"

"No. That's the problem. There's absolutely nothing to indicate that such a dramatic transformation should have happened. They have the same leadership, no internal struggles that we've heard about, and the Zatoras haven't done anything we know of to provoke a response. They did attack some dealers and leave some bodies, but that's not too far out of the ordinary. Unfortunately."

Cali wracked her brain but came up empty. "I have nothing. The last...uh, incident seemed to be normal." She wasn't sure how much detail to give the other woman about her ongoing conflict with the Atlanteans despite having called her for help during the first battle. It was hard to know where one stood with Detective Kendra Barton. "And I haven't heard or seen anything since." She hadn't mentioned the watchers from earlier in the day to anyone and didn't think it had any relevance to the discussion.

"Yeah. And that's the word all over. They've made this

big change and there's no information coming out. But the folks we're interfaced with say it could very well be a prelude to something major."

She stiffened in her chair. "Like what?"

The woman raised her hands, palms up, then lowered them. "Who the hell knows? My money is on a move against the Zatoras, but it doesn't seem like they're fully ready for that. Unless the Atlanteans had a sudden influx of people we're unaware of, the humans still have more boots on the ground in the city."

"But they did try the operation at the docks. It had to be aimed at the other gang, true?"

Barton nodded. "Yeah, there's that. But still, it simply doesn't sit right with me. There's something else happening here."

"So what's your plan?" Zeb asked.

After a long, slow sip, the detective put the glass down gently as if she had to resist the urge to shatter it on the top of the bar. "Honestly, I don't have one, which is why I'm here. I hoped that either of you or your buddy Shale might have something to add to the evidence." Her use of Tanyith's last name was a game at this point, an echo of the initial distrust that had clearly faded over time.

Cali shook her head. "I have nothing. Seriously. The Atlanteans haven't so much as peeped at me since the last time."

The dwarf spoke unexpectedly. "Vizidus sent word that rumors are circulating in several of the magical communities. These speak of something dire and dramatic to come in the imminent future."

Barton's head snapped toward him. "When? What?

Where?"

He sighed. "I asked the same questions and in much the same way. No more information is available. I requested that he put the word out to everyone to see if we can find anything else out, but I'm not hopeful. Whatever it might be, it seems like someone is doing their best to ensure the secret doesn't get out before it happens."

The woman slapped her open palms on the bar and yelled, "Damn it." She pulled her anger back and continued more calmly, "Okay. I can talk to the bosses and see if they'll approve some overtime. We can put more people on the streets and start leaning on the informants we have—all of them, regardless of who they're connected to. Maybe we'll get lucky. What can you two do?"

Zeb shrugged. "There's not much more I can offer than passing word back and forth and providing a refuge for anyone who needs it."

The last part of his statement reminded her of something. "Tanyith could probably get word to the people who helped at the docks. The ones in the helicopters." As far as she knew, Barton wasn't fully in the loop on the magical agents who had visited.

The detective stared at her like she knew secrets were being kept from her and didn't like it. *Or maybe that's only my guilty conscience.* She finally said, "Yeah, we should try everything. Let him know. Maybe they have something on it."

Cali once again thought hard for something else she could add or do but didn't come up with anything. "Of course, I'll keep my ears open too, but I don't really have connections. Not like you all."

The woman sighed. "Hopefully, it's not one of the worst-case scenarios Shale and I discussed at the start of the drug push. I'd hate to see the city caught in an epidemic."

The dwarf looked concerned. "Did you analyze a sample of the stuff they're peddling?"

She nodded. "The feds did. The one they're passing out to magicals has—get this—magical things in it. Apparently, they do something to the metabolism and the brain. I don't understand it but it's at the level that a high-end narcotic would be to a human."

Cali hissed in a sharp breath. "Damn. That sounds scary."

"Not as scary as the human one. It has a really strange set of ingredients, including traditional drugs we've heard of, something synthetic they've never seen that seems to act as a hallucinogen, and something inert they don't comprehend at all."

"So that's why you're worried about epidemics—because of the last thing?"

She nodded. "You got it in one. That, and the fact that they're pushing so hard. If they were after money only, there are other ways to get it that are as easy, so you'd think they'd do those too."

The girl frowned when something occurred to her. "Taking customers away from the Zatoras? Maybe that's it?"

Barton finished her drink in a long gulp. "It could be. But, again, they're investing so much energy into it that...I don't know. It feels bigger."

"And you think this is the thing that everyone's worried about?"

The detective stood and stretched her hands high into the air, then rolled her neck with a cracking sound. "That's the heart of the matter. If it is what they're talking about, that's certainly bad. Maybe even really bad. But what if it's not? What could be more concerning than what we've come up with? That's what wakes me up at three in the morning in a cold sweat." She patted Cali awkwardly on the shoulder as she passed and was out the door without another word.

Zeb met her gaze, and she thought the look on his face seemed as concerned as she felt, which was very concerned. "What do you think?"

The dwarf shook his head. "I don't know. And I hate not knowing."

She laughed. "Welcome to every day of my existence."

He didn't react to the joke. "You be careful—and I mean extra careful. Carry a second healing potion with you wherever you go." He looked at the Draksa. "From here on out, you're with her everywhere, got it?" He apparently received the response he wanted because he looked up again. "Both of you keep your eyes open. Like it or not, you're in the middle of this, so you might see something coming before anyone else does."

Cali sighed. *No pressure. Only, you know, potentially the fate of the city.* "Thanks for the reassurance, boss."

This time, he did smile. "Anytime. Now, go lock the door and get home to get some sleep. Something tells me we'll all need every hour of rest we can manage."

CHAPTER NINETEEN

For once, Cali had taken Zeb's advice and slept in. She even ignored Fyre's cold-nosed attempts to get her up for a training session. He'd eventually given up and crawled on top of the covers beside her, and they'd rested until noon. By the time she finally arrived at the Dragons, it was almost two pm. She climbed the stairs from the basement to find the tavern mostly empty, and Fyre dashed past her to take his accustomed place behind the bar. During the midday lull, Zeb saw to the customers himself since Janice was taking afternoon art classes. She was glad she'd missed having to see the tavern's other server.

Tanyith had arrived before her and seemed to be thoroughly enjoying a bowl of something from the stewpot. She noted that he'd begun to keep Nylotte's leather jacket gift with him at all times, exactly like she did when she wasn't going to or from the dojo. It never hurt to be prepared. She didn't bother to check what the recipe of the day was as she tried not to eat until immediately before her shift so she'd have the energy to push through it. There was rarely enough downtime to snack during the night, although on occasion, she'd been known to carry a fork and stab pieces of meat out of the bowls of people who annoyed her.

She threw her backpack on one of the long common tables with a groan and sat with her jeans-covered legs tucked beneath her. Today's concert t-shirt was a good one from the first Lollapalooza. It always invoked comments, often negative ones that led to arguments that were usually entertaining for everyone involved. She folded her laptop open and accessed the textbook for her criminal behavior class. The case study parts of the course were far more enjoyable than the theory behind it all. *When it comes right down to it, I'm more interested in doing things than thinking about things, I guess.*

In a pleasant turn of events, Tanyith brought a soft cider over and set the glass on the table beside her, then returned to his place at the bar. If her eavesdropping skills were up to snuff, he and her boss were discussing whether the current quarterback of the Saints could be counted on for another year if they didn't make the Superbowl. While she liked sports as much as most reasonable people, talking about it was always a snoozer for her. *Maybe not as exhausting as this stuff, though.*

She read the same page for the third time, sighed, and slammed the book closed. The bench creaked as she pushed herself off it and went to stand beside Tay. "Did you tell him he missed seeing Detective Barton?"

Zeb nodded, and she turned to face the other man. "Kendra asked about you. Seriously, are you two dating or merely using each other for a little stress release? You can tell us." He groaned, the dwarf laughed, and she grinned widely.

After several seconds of staring at the ceiling like someone above would deliver him from her accusations, he replied, "None of the above." He lowered his head to look at her. "Zeb told me what you discussed. Scary stuff."

Well. Way to kill the mood. "Yeah, it is. Definitely. Have you heard anything?"

"No, but I passed the word to Nylotte like you asked." She'd texted him the night before with the request. "There's no answer yet."

"Dang it." She sighed. "I'm really not into this homework thing today. I should have gone out training with the beast over there."

Zeb shook his head. "Work before play."

She laughed. "Training is work, these days. It doesn't pay well, obviously, but it also ensures I don't have my ass handed to me by random attacks or Atlantean enforcers. Speaking of which, Tanyith, I need you to be my third. Zeb won't bring Valerie out of retirement for me."

"Sure." He turned to face the bartender. "What is your deal, anyway? Every other dwarf I've known would have jumped at the chance for a fight. Any fight." It was more tease than a question.

Unexpectedly, Zeb answered. "I've done enough fighting for at least three other people. It was time to be finished." The reply was more than she'd ever heard from him on the topic and the depth of emotion with which he said it was as surprising as the answer.

Tanyith nodded. "Gotcha." The heavy emotion behind the dwarf's statement hung uncomfortably, and he focused on his food. She slid off the stool and headed to her table to focus on her studies. They passed a quarter of an hour in comfortable silence, and she had begun to think she might actually get her homework done early when suddenly, Fyre growled and leapt up to stand on the bar.

It was so unexpected that they all stared at him for several seconds until they heard boots pounding on the stairs. Nylotte burst into the room and stopped facing them. She seemed to be dressed for battle in leather pants, heavy boots, and a version of the coats she'd given them. Her hair was bound into a warrior's braid at the base of her neck and the expression on her face was fierce and angry. "You two, come with me." She pointed at Zeb. "Get your council. Get your magicals. Get everyone who can sling a spell. Hell, call the damn National Guard. We have a situation."

A minute later, Tanyith, Cali, and Fyre followed the Drow through the portal she'd created and stepped onto the docks that had been the location of the cruise ship battle. Those who had them had donned and zipped their protective jackets. Zeb was contacting everyone he knew for assistance, including Barton whom he would request to muster a human response to the situation.

The Dark Elf had explained that an attack of some kind was imminent and that it would come from the water, but nothing more. No sign of any threat was visible, and the sun shone in a cloudless sky. Cali lifted a hand to shade her eyes and looked in all directions. "So, how about a few details?"

Nylotte growled with irritation and impatience. "One minute." She cast a spell to amplify her voice and yelled, "Clear the docks. This is not a drill. Everyone move!" Workers scattered at her words, doubtless aware of what had happened there before. She shook her head and surveyed the water carefully. "Okay, so, the chief tech for the agents contacted me. She and her counterpart have access to most of the satellites with cameras, and they programmed some kind of computer whatever to watch for trouble in a circle starting from Atlantis and stretching to here and Texas."

"Why Texas?" Tanyith asked.

The woman scowled. "Why not Texas? I don't know because I don't ask stupid questions. Anyway, they detected a fast-moving object leaving Atlantis, and it looks like this will be its destination."

Cali risked her displeasure. "How fast?"

"Really fast." She nodded grimly. "Less than an hour to get from there to here, if it takes the most direct route. But it went deep—too deep to be seen—so we're not sure. We won't know until it gets closer to the surface."

"Why didn't we have more warning?"

The Drow sighed. "They tried to push it up their chain of command first and only contacted me after they couldn't reach her. That means precious time was lost." She shook her head. "The magicals among the agents are on the other planet at the moment and apparently, whatever communication system they thought they had was inadequate."

Tanyith asked, "Why didn't you go get them?"

"It's technically not their problem, but more importantly, I don't know where they are and it would have taken too long to find them. Hopefully, your bartender friend will be able to muster some support for us." She sounded less confident than Cali had ever heard her be, and she realized an important question hadn't been addressed.

"So…uh, what is it? You said 'a fast-moving object.' Do you know any more than that?"

Nylotte laughed. "We didn't actually have visual, so we can't be sure. But they ran displacement analysis on the water patterns it made. It's big."

The question had to be asked, even though she really didn't want to know the answer. "How big?"

"Too damn big. Like, the size of a small office building. Five stories or so."

Tanyith's breath caught. "Holy hell. And it's coming here—why?"

"Probably not to talk."

Cali squeezed her eyes shut but when she opened them, she still stood on the docks so her hope that it might be a dream was dashed. She looked left at a strange sound and startled when portals opened. Wizards, witches, Kilomea, and Light and Dark Elves emerged from them, at least a handful of each. She recognized the leaders of each group as council members, and they gathered together and headed toward her as their people spread out.

The wizard, Vizidus, stopped a few feet away and asked, "I hear we have a situation?"

The Drow replied, "Something's coming. And it's big. What will the response look like from you all?"

He pushed stray strands of his long white hair out of his face. "Our main people are here already, with a few others rallying more. Zeb told me to tell you that 'the detective is on it,' whatever that means."

Cali exchanged looks with Tanyith, but she passed on teasing him about Barton. The gravity of the moment increased second by second. A buzzing sound came from somewhere, and Nylotte pulled a phone out of one of the pockets of her jacket. "Go," she snapped, nodded several times, and stored the cell.

"It's now close enough to the surface to be trackable. They estimate we have three minutes. Let's spread out so that whatever it is can't attack us all at once." The council members turned and began to direct their people to move, while she jogged toward one end of the docks.

They followed, and Tanyith said, "Please tell me we're moving away from where it'll appear."

Nylotte shook her head and her braid danced from side to side. "Of course not. There's nothing to gain by hiding. We need to strike whatever it is hard and maintain our attack it until it goes away. If we're lucky, it's something that can be convinced to leave if it's losing."

"And if we're not lucky?" Cali asked.

"Then there will be far fewer people in New Orleans tomorrow than there are today if we don't do our jobs and defeat it."

Tanyith chuckled. "Does trouble follow you everywhere?"

"Hardly," the Dark Elf replied. "It's the other way around."

With a sound much like waves breaking against a cliff, the water erupted in the river before them and surged to sweep over the concrete of the dock area. Shields shimmered into being as the waiting magicals defended themselves against it. When the spray had cleared enough that she could see, Cali was almost unable to accept the evidence before her.

She'd heard of such a thing, of course, but it was mythological. Her brain babbled, "Not real, not real, not real," in an unending loop, and she tried to form words. Finally, she managed to unclench her jaw enough to ask, "Is that a Leviathan?"

Her partner's voice shook slightly when he answered her. "No, a Leviathan is more like a sea dragon. That right there is an oversized octopus, which makes it a Kraken."

Nylotte sighed. "And since it doesn't exist naturally, someone created it—and logically did so for a purpose. And you know what that means." The giant creature towered above them, whipped its tentacles in the air, and roared its fury at the small figures before it.

"Yeah," Cali said. "We didn't get lucky and it's here to kill us all."

The Drow nodded and shouted a hoarse battle cry as she raised her hands to attack.

CHAPTER TWENTY

The creature was enormous, the largest living thing Cali had ever seen by far. She was rooted to the ground before it and could only stare as the tentacles whipped viciously. Nylotte's bellow jolted her from her reverie in time to add her magic to the barrage of force bolts, fire, ice, lighting, and shadow that pounded into the monster from all over the dock.

Each attack found purchase but seemingly accomplished nothing. Under such an intense assault of power, she would have expected the creature to at least flinch away, perhaps reconsider what it was doing, and nip off to snack on several schools of fish or something. Rather than show any concern, however, it retaliated.

A tentacle as long as four or five tractor-trailers back to back and twice as tall whipped across the dock from her right. She shouted to warn Tanyith and Nylotte and blasted herself upward with force magic barely in time for it to pass below her. Although she landed almost immediately, she had to repeat the action with the one that followed. Screams and shouts from farther down the docks indicated that not everyone had managed to avoid it. *Damn it. How are we supposed to defeat a building-sized enemy with eight arms?*

She checked to be sure a third wasn't on the way, then turned to examine the damage. Several beings had fallen but she couldn't tell which group they came from. A pack of Kilomea with sharp weapons battled the first appendage, which reared and slapped in an attempt to strike them. One of the giants managed to plant a spear, and the Kraken impaled its thrashing limb on the metal spike. The creature screamed in rage and three other tentacles swung onto the same place to annihilate the huge warriors. When they raised, the victims didn't move, their bodies crushed beneath the enormous weight of the limb.

Cali shouted, "So, one strike and you're dead—one-shot city. Don't get hit."

Tanyith growled annoyance. "I'm doing my best." He fired shadow bolts at the creature's eyes but they deflected from its eyelids, which were almost closed to protect the vulnerable flesh beneath. She added her attacks to the same area but they failed to penetrate. The Drow had run closer to the creature to attempt a better angle, but her shadow blasts didn't accomplish any more than their efforts had. The Kraken swung another tentacle across the docks, which forced them all to take evasive action, then whirled a different one from above. The appendage pounded into the terminal building that ran along the full length of the dock and caved the roof in, and bricks and debris erupted in all directions.

Cali dashed up beside Nylotte and tried to target the

same areas she was. She had to yell to be heard over the thrashing water, the shouts of attackers, the shrieks of the Kraken, and the cries of pain. "We don't seem to have inflicted any injuries."

The Dark Elf shook her head. "We need to coordinate our attacks. You and Tanyith go tell everyone to take their lead from me. No is not an acceptable answer."

She nodded and sent a telepathic message to Fyre—who had swooped in repeatedly to breathe frost at the beast's face without significant effect—and told him to assist Nylotte and keep her safe. His acknowledgment was colored with irritation, but that was fine as long as he did it. The Draksa was a warrior and didn't like to be taken out of the fight for any reason, but he was hopefully also smart enough to know he couldn't defeat the giant octopus alone.

Her focus now on the task at hand, she sprinted to Tanyith and caught his arm to drag him along as she ran toward the others. "Tell everyone to follow Nylotte's lead!" He nodded, and she pushed him at the wizards and witches, then raced to the Light Elves who were closest. She recognized Malonne from Zeb's descriptions, but he had a lash mark across his cheek that was raw and bleeding, and his eyes were filled with anger. She yelled, "Do what Nylotte does," and pointed at her. He looked like he would refuse, then turned and gestured his people forward toward where the Dark Elf dodged in and out between strikes from the Kraken's tentacles.

Once satisfied that they would cooperate, she delivered the same message to the remaining Kilomea and to the Dark Elves, then rushed to rejoin the battle. She reached it in time to take a blow from one of the sweeping limbs. The force sent her into a sprawl and she screamed, "*Aspida*," to invoke the shield charm her parents had left her. The huge column of octopus flesh raised high above her and hammered down, and she curled in desperate fear as it made impact.

Thankfully, the shield held. When the tentacle departed to seek other prey, she rose to her feet, unharmed and angry. "Okay, you stupid excuse for a sea creature. It's time to go back to where you came from." She darted into a corner of the warehouse building that was still standing and sent her mind out toward the Kraken's.

She sensed it easily as its mental presence was as enormous as its physical one. Her sweep also brought the emotions of her allies to her, fear and pain the most common. She pushed them away and tried to pierce the monster's mind, only to discover a barrier around it, too thick and strong for her to overcome. Another attempt failed and the one after did as well. "I don't know what that means, but I bet it's not good," she muttered darkly and decided not to pursue the useless effort.

When she moved closer to Nylotte, the Dark Elf was shouting orders. "We have to target the eyes. Everyone needs to attack at once. Electricity first, then fire, then the rest. Let's see if we can sneak in around the edges before it closes them." Heads nodded all round as the collected group continued to launch their assaults. "If it attacks, shield, evade, and come back to it. We'll keep doing it until it works or we think of something better."

A tentacle swept across, then lifted and drove down almost without warning. The group scattered to avoid it, except for a witch who failed to get out of the way in time and was crushed and two Dark Elves who summoned shields to protect themselves. The group managed a single barrage keyed off the Drow's attack and fired at the left eye before two tentacles swept viciously in a combined assault that made them break formation and bolt to safety.

She stepped up beside Nylotte, who seemed to take the creature's attempts to hurt them as a personal affront. The elf yelled, "I couldn't get into its mind to convince it to leave, and its hide is insanely thick. It's not normal."

Well, at least I'm not the only one who failed with mental magic. Cali laughed, and if a note of growing hysteria was mixed into the sound, she wasn't embarrassed by it. "As if anything about that gigantic monstrosity could be normal."

"True enough. Let's get to it." Her companion surged forward, and the girl ran at her heels. She called to Fyre with her mind and instructed him to try to distract their adversary as Nylotte signaled an attack. A flood of approval from him washed over her. She sensed him swoop overhead but he maintained his veil, which she presumed meant the obscenely large octopus couldn't see through it. Unfortunately, his frost attacks inflicted as little injury as any of their other assaults did.

A thought occurred to her as they launched yet another barrage of magical power at the Kraken and failed utterly to penetrate its thick hide. She avoided the next two appendages and ran to Tanyith's side. He greeted her with a dark laugh. "So, this is fun."

She nodded. "Are you okay?" He had a gash across his forehead that was bloody but not actively bleeding.

"Yeah. It was only flying shrapnel from the stupid building."

"I have an idea, but I wanted to make sure it wasn't insane first."

His laugh had actual humor in it this time. "Well, if it's yours, I have my doubts going in. But let's hear it."

Cali flipped him off. "We can't penetrate its skin, so we need to cut it so the magic can get to something more tender. Maybe all it will take is a single breach to make it happen, you know?"

The Kraken screeched and battered its tentacles into the warehouse building again. The people on the dock shielded, dove for cover, or took damage from the shrapnel. Tanyith cursed. "That beast is much smarter than the average octopus."

"You think? Really?" She shook her head to try to get rid of the water that dripped into her eyes. "So, what about my plan?"

"I love it. How do we cut it?"

"I hadn't thought that far ahead but I bet Nylotte will know, though."

She blew out a breath, turned, and ran toward the Drow but only made it halfway there before the concussion from a large explosion swept her off her feet and she careened helplessly, entirely airborne. She collided with several others and they all crumpled in a heap against one of the remaining walls of the warehouse.

The person on the top, a thin witch who wore motorcycle leathers, groaned. "Hey, the humans are here. And they've brought rockets. That should make things way better."

CHAPTER TWENTY-ONE

The tangled pile of magicals quickly and carefully unstacked themselves and a minute later, Cali was on her feet again. She was bruised and battered but otherwise whole. Others had recovered from the blast faster or weathered it somehow because the fight against the monster octopus was still going strong.

The Kraken had taken notice of the newcomers and swiped two Humvees with machine guns away. They now burned at the far end of the docks, and everyone who had been positioned on that side had wisely moved toward the center. The remaining vehicles retreated to the edges and discharged soldiers with impressive-looking weapons.

She added her force magic to the attacks and sent a mental message to Fyre to assure him she was fine. When the pressure let up in her head, she realized he must have tried to contact her. *Not telepathy, but definitely a connection.* Her amazement at the Draksa's abilities inched a touch higher.

Even with the addition of the bullets, grenades, and

rockets, they didn't seem to actually penetrate the thick hide. She hurried up beside Nylotte and said as much, and the Dark Elf nodded as she fired thin lines of shadow at the creature. Her voice was hoarse and her clothes and hair were drenched and dripping. "It stands to reason it will require magic to pierce its skin since its nature is magical. But we're running out of options to try."

Tanyith stepped up on the other side of the Drow. "I'm completely out of ideas. I feel like we're merely flailing away at this damn bastard. At least it's stuck in the water."

The elf shook her head emphatically. "It's not. We're holding it here. If whoever created it managed this much, they surely made it possible for it to fight on land."

At that, he looked sick. "So this monstrosity could crawl through the French Quarter if we lose?"

She nodded. "Exactly that. So we mustn't fail."

"Maybe it's time you jumped to the other planet to summon your friends to the rescue again," Cali suggested

The Dark Elf barked a frustrated laugh. "Believe me, I tried that before I came to get you folks. They're hidden from me. I'm sure they're fine, but wherever they are, it blocks my ability to detect them. There are many places like that on Oriceran, unfortunately."

They all dealt with the tentacle that assaulted their position in different ways. Tanyith launched himself up with a force burst and moved to the side of the mammoth limb. Cali ran, then dove and rolled and barely managed to avoid it as it thumped onto the concrete surface of the docks. Nylotte shielded herself and the wall of flesh didn't touch her. When the appendage pulled away to cause more mayhem elsewhere, she was still standing and began to attack again. "The Kilomea hurt the bastard earlier," she shouted, They must have a magic weapon that was strong enough to work. Go and find it."

Cali turned and ran, thankful that she made time for morning runs so that she could sprint down the docks again and know she'd be able to fight thereafter. On top of the warehouse building, Light and Dark elves fired actual arrows from long ornate bows, but even when they managed to get through the waving limbs, they simply stuck in its hide. *They must be magical if they accomplish that much.*

The crushed bodies of the Kilomean contingent were a short distance ahead, and she had almost reached them when a giant tentacle thwacked on the ground in front of her to cut her off from them. She cursed under her breath and punched at the barrier with fists of force that had no effect. "Move, you ugly beast," she muttered. It seemed as if the creature knew what she'd intended to do and had determined to stop her.

Cali activated her sticks and pounded furiously on the limb but again, the attack accomplished nothing. She cursed. "It sure would be nice to have a magic sword right about now." Her jaw fell open in surprise when the black sticks with the red etchings transformed into blades, the edges so sharp they seemed to glow when the sun caught them. Her brain stopped working, stunned by the development, but her body, fortunately, didn't. She sliced at the appendage and the creature pulled it back with a screech, which gave her access to the Kilomeas' magical weapon.

Quickly, she converted her left weapon into a bracelet once more, grasped the spear in that hand, then turned and raced toward the Dark elf again. When she arrived, she immediately shared her discovery. "Magical blades can cut it."

Nylotte took the spear. "That's good to know. Now to make this weapon count."

She had assumed that the Drow simply wanted to replicate the earlier tactic and let the monster's tentacles impale themselves on it, but she clearly had something else in mind as she ceased her attacks. She summoned a shield in her left hand, a body-high shimmering force field that wrapped around her on both sides and the top, almost like half a cocoon. Cali stored the idea of the insanely practical defense into a corner of her mind so she could learn to copy it later when an enormous octopus wasn't gleefully trying to destroy her city. *Assuming there is a later.*

The elf swayed from side to side with the spear in a throwing position, clearly waiting for the creature to present her with a target. *What she needs is a distraction.* She put her hand on Nylotte's shoulder and yelled, "Hold on a second. We can give that monster something else to worry about." She sent a message to Fyre. "You need to distract it. Get in there and claw it or something and make sure it sees you coming. But don't you dare get hurt." Acceptance and amusement flickered across the connection between them, and a slight shimmer in the air overhead resolved into the form of the Draksa, who now climbed in a spiral.

The Kraken saw him immediately and shrieked with rage, but Fyre was out of range of the grasping tentacles for the moment. The Dark Elf yelled, "Good plan," and called to those near her. "Pass the word. When it takes a wound, direct everything you have to the point of injury.

Tanyith, go and tell the humans." He looked like he would argue, then sprinted away. She was close enough to hear the Drow chuckle and murmur, "If only all the people I work with would be so practical."

Cali banished her second stick and readied her power. It was there, waiting for her call and anxious to be released. The surrounding battle slowed as her brain latched onto a thought and refused to let it go. *It's another metaphor. All this time, I've thought of my magic as a reservoir or a pool, something that needs to be drawn from and replenished. Maybe that's what it was when I was under my parents' magical restriction, but not anymore.* The sensation of power was present in every cell and she was full to bursting with it. *It's not about pulling my magic up and sending it out. It's already present all through my body. I simply need to let it flow.*

Above her, Fyre sounded a battle cry and dove, his wings folded tightly against his body. He arrowed toward the Kraken and flicked his tail and wings when needed to avoid the tentacles that sought him. He aimed for the head, and Nylotte's arm shifted slightly to target the creature's eye. Around them, magic blasted, the chatter of machine guns sounded, and rockets continued to impact into the creature with concussive force, but it was all background noise to the drama that played out before here.

The Draksa curved his trajectory as he reached the monster, extended his talons, and scraped them across the massive forehead. Its protective shell parted and ichor belched from the wound. Nylotte's spear was already in the air, and it narrowly missed the dragon lizard as it rocketed past to plunge into the monstrous octopus. The beast howled in pain, the weapon buried to three-quarters of its length in its eye.

"Now—everything!" Nylotte screamed, and Cali hurtled fire down an imaginary line that connected her hands to the wound on the monster's forehead. Her magic copied the shape of the chasm Fyre had created and stretched to encompass the entire opening at once. This time, the Kraken's screech sounded like fear, and it continued to scream as it writhed in clear agony under the angry barrage that had finally found a vulnerability to exploit.

Fyre darted in again and added his own frost attack to the magical fusillade, and she blasted the ice with force to turn it into shards that plunged deeper into the creature. The Draksa rolled and climbed for another strike. Tanyith had returned and fired his own blasts of power at their foe to wreathe the open wounds in lightning that stabbed deep within.

When the killing blow struck, it was a surprise to everyone. One of the humans fired a shoulder-mounted rocket and it drilled into the cavity that had been created where the spear had pierced its eye. The muffled sound of a detonation from inside the giant skull preceded its collapse. The enormous head and body thrashed violently, then surged onto the dock. Its weight and ferocious struggles destroyed the center portion entirely and dropped it into the water, along with the defenders who had been positioned there. As the Kraken sunk, the people still on the dock raced to rescue those who had been injured by the creature's death throes.

Cali raced toward the center and shouted in her head for Fyre to assist. The request was unnecessary, as he was already rising from the water with a Light Elf in his claws and carried the wounded magical to safety. She'd never imagined that the scene ahead could be possible. Magicals of one group helped those of the others without concern for the various issues that usually divided them. Even amidst the chaos, the sight made something inside her shout with triumph. This was how things ought to be all the time.

An hour later, the rescues were complete, the wounded had been stabilized and transported, and most of those who had risen to the responsibility of protecting the city had portaled away. Nylotte had vanished quickly after the situation became stable, saying she needed to check on her student and let her know what had happened, assuming she could find her. Cali and Tanyith sat on the concrete, wrapped in blankets, with Fyre the Rottweiler at her side. She recognized the boots before she managed to summon the energy to look up. When she did finally raise her eyes, she saw a disheveled woman with a cut on her cheek and a red-stained bandage tied around one bicep.

"Detective Barton. Have you come to check on your boyfriend?"

She laughed. "He only wishes he was my boyfriend. What do you know about this situation? I have all kinds of information on what happened but no idea why it happened. Is there any chance you have a line on that?"

Cali looked at Tanyith, who shook his head. She replied, "It's incredibly frustrating to admit this, but I know nothing. Our involvement started when the alert went out about something happening at the docks. We came here and joined the battle. It's nice that you were able to join us, though. And even nicer that you brought friends with big guns."

Barton sighed. "Yeah, big guns that were basically useless until you all used your magic. It's kind of frightening to think that without a group of civilians, we'd have a ludicrous mythological sea creature crawling through the streets right now."

"Maybe New Orleans should have one of those special SWAT teams. What are they called?"

"AET. Do you know how expensive those are?"

Cali laughed. "More expensive than rebuilding the French Quarter?"

"Point taken." She shook her head. "Are you sure you don't know anything else?" The frustration was clear in her expression, but unlike previous versions, this one didn't seem to be directed specifically at her.

"No. Honestly, I'd tell you if I could. I don't like the looks of this any more than you do. But I will mention one thing I noticed."

An eager look crept in around the edges of the woman's frown. "What's that?"

"If I was in a gang and a sea creature attacked my city, I'd take a hand in its defense. But I didn't see a single Atlantean here. Which makes me think that, at the very least, they were cool with whatever resulted from the situation."

The detective nodded. "That's a good point."

She sighed. "So, is this the part where we start looking for someone to create our own giant monsters so we can fight things like this? What was it—Mecha-Godzilla?"

Barton laughed. "If we can't afford AET, we certainly won't be able to manage that."

"Toy robots with grenades wired to them?"

"Maybe."

"Good. Good. Problem solved."

The woman walked away, shaking her head. Cali was sure there'd been an actual smile before she departed. She did the only thing that was left to do and turned to face Tanyith. "So, lover boy, you missed another chance to ask her out. Seriously, right after a major scare is prime time according to the movies. Will you actually get your act together one of these days, or do I need to do it for you?"

CHAPTER TWENTY-TWO

Even though she was exhausted from the battle, Cali had returned to the tavern to work the night before, knowing she'd be too keyed up to sleep. Fyre had made it to the back of the bar, collapsed, and snored the evening away until she woke him to head home.

Zeb had given her the day off citing that a monster attack on the city was a reasonable cause, and she'd spent it sleeping until his text roused her at five pm. *Council meeting, your presence requested. Here, eleven o'clock.* She sighed and fell asleep until the absolute last minute, then threw on her nicest jeans and t-shirt combination and portaled over with Fyre at her side.

Her boss was descending the stairs to the basement when she arrived. He growled in irritation. "Have you ever heard of being early?"

"Have you ever heard of not being a whiny jerk?" she snarked in rebuttal.

He laughed, and she walked forward and hugged him. For a moment, he stiffened, but relaxed and patted her awkwardly on the back. She broke the embrace and stepped away. His perplexed look made her laugh, and his irritation at her laughter only increased it. After a few seconds, she mastered herself. "After yesterday, I realized that danger is everywhere and you don't know what'll happen at any given moment. So, I've decided to become a hugger."

His face scrunched in doubt. "A hugger."

"Yes. One who hugs."

"Trees?"

She shrugged. "Sure. Trees. Dwarves. Draksa. Maybe even Barton."

"Oh, that's a reaction I'd love to see." He laughed.

Cali grinned. "I bet Tanyith would be jealous."

Zeb tilted his head slightly to the side. "You really think there's something there, don't you? You're not simply being a twit."

She pointed a finger at him. "First, I am never, ever, simply a twit. A twit is only part of what I am. And yes, I do. In the beginning, I only screwed around, but have you seen the way they look at each other?"

He folded his arms and stared at her. "Suspiciously?"

"No." She mimicked his posture and stared in return. "Interested-like. How long has it been since you've had a date, anyway?" She'd never seen him with another dwarf at the tavern and never seen him at all outside its walls. *Maybe he's a ghost, doomed to haunt the place and we can all see dead people.*

Zeb lowered his arms and moved to the center of the room. "That is none of your business. But more recently than you, I would guess."

She shook her head and replied, "I'm totally in demand." Fyre snorted, and she rounded on him and held a fist up. "Quiet you, or you're gonna find yourself bopped on the nose with extreme prejudice." A combined scraping and crashing sound came from nearby, and she turned as several crates slid out of the way to provide access to one of the room's walls. "Wait. I thought you were coming down here to get supplies. What are you doing?"

The dwarf grinned over his shoulder. "You think you know it all, but in reality, not so much." He placed his hands on the wall and muttered something she couldn't make out, and the brick surface moved back, then slid off to the side to create a wide doorway and reveal the room behind it.

Cali walked through the entrance and looked around. To her right were several small casks, identical in size to the one for his custom brew upstairs. A cupboard stood against the wall beyond them, a fireplace on the left, and a large round table in the center with seven chairs. Zeb waved and seven glasses floated out of the cupboard and landed in the proper position.

He pointed at the stone fireplace. "Start a fire. Let's make this place a little less moist." She approached to a safer distance and dispatched an orange line of flame into the wood that was stacked inside. The smaller pieces caught quickly, and she turned to face her boss.

"So, this was here the whole time and you didn't think it was important to share that with me."

"You didn't have a reason to know. Now, you do."

"How about honesty, for one? Maybe you've heard of it?"

Zeb merely laughed at her sarcasm. "Right. Like you're honest with Barton. A real paragon of virtue, you."

"Touché, old man. You'll get it for that. Just you wait." She walked to the cupboard and retrieved a glass for herself since he'd rudely not included one for her. The council numbered seven, and thus the seven chairs, which meant she'd stand for the evening meeting, which was fine. "What's in the casks?"

He pointed to each in turn. "Red wine. White wine. Mulled cider—a special batch with extra honey."

She drew some and tasted it. Although a little potent, it was nothing like his stash upstairs. Still, given her constitution, she'd limit herself to sipping one for the flavor.

"So what's the deal with this place?"

Her boss turned from where he was doing something at the far end of the room. He shrugged as he walked toward her. "They needed a neutral location to meet and I had already built this area for storage. I thought I might do some whiskey distilling at some point. But I realized it'd make kind of a nice clubhouse, so that's what I did."

"A clubhouse."

"Yep."

"For a group of grown men."

"And women."

She rolled her eyes. "That makes it all better. Thanks for the clarification."

He sighed. "Okay, perhaps I thought it was cool having a secret place. And maybe, just maybe, it's also a safe room in case everything goes to hell."

Cali frowned. "And why would you need one of those?"

Zeb shook his head. "I haven't always been a bartender,

girl. And I'm well aware of the dangers that are present out in the allegedly civilized city we live in."

Of course, she immediately wanted to continue that line of questioning in the worst way, but a portal opened and terminated the conversation. Malonne stepped through, his wounds from the battle healed. He greeted her first, then Zeb, and moved directly to the casks with a glass in hand. The other council members arrived one by one and before too long, everyone was in a seat except for Cali, who stood behind the one her boss selected.

The gathering turned expectantly toward the wizard, and he smiled at her. "Caliste, thank you for coming."

"You're welcome. Thanks for inviting me to your clubhouse," she quipped.

Silence hung for a long moment before the witch beside him began to laugh and soon, most of the others at the table joined her. Vizidus only grinned but didn't seem offended in the least. "You, also, are welcome. I assume you know everyone at the table?"

She nodded. "Not necessarily in person, but Zeb has told me about you all."

Delia chuckled. "Hopefully, only good things."

Cali raised an eyebrow. "About the others, sure, but about you, well, uh…yeah."

"I like this one." The witch laughed. "She has fire."

She sent a mental message to the Draksa, who hid beneath a veil and behind some boxes in the basement. "Indeed I do." He returned amusement to her. Out loud, she said, "I try. Zeb loves it."

More laughter greeted that until Vizidus rapped his knuckles on the table. "All amusing wordplay aside, we are here for a reason, so let's get to it. Delia, please begin."

The witch nodded. "Caliste, do you know anything about what the hell caused the chaos at the docks the other day?"

She laughed at the directness of her question. "Call me Cali, everyone, please. And I don't have any more information than you do, except that it came from New Atlantis and had a seriously bad attitude."

"How did you know how to defeat it?" the Kilomea asked.

Cali shook her head. "I didn't. Your people were the first to hurt it when they stabbed it with the spear. That gave me the thought that maybe only enchanted weapons could damage its skin and that it was somehow spell-proof. Although Fyre's claws apparently count too."

Scoppic smiled at her. "I wasn't there, but I did see the recording that the news station played. Your companion was magnificent." Zeb had dutifully informed the council about the Draksa when the creature had adopted her and had told her that he'd done so some time later.

"He was. He always is. Thank you for saying so."

Malonne asked, "Is there really nothing more you can share about what's going on since you seem to be at the center of it all?"

Zeb replied for her. "You've all heard the reports I've shared. We haven't held anything back. What are you getting at, exactly?"

Invel sighed. "What a couple of my colleagues are wondering is if Caliste isn't somehow more than she has revealed to us. Why has the Atlantean gang targeted her?

Why is this city suddenly so important that it's worth sending a horrific creature to attack it? There seems to be a storm of unexpected events and they swirl around as if drawn to her."

Cali laughed, but it was helplessness rather than humor. "I really, really wish I knew but I don't. Perhaps if I survive the next battle, I'll ask them."

Scoppic spoke out of turn, as she understood the rules, which seemed to shock the whole table. "You could do that, in fact. I had a little free time, so I did some research about the trials. The victor may request a boon, and if it is within the defeated champion's ability to give it, they are obligated to do so. If the champion cannot, the person the champion represents shares an identical obligation. It doesn't go beyond that, but if the gang's secondary leader is attending, you might be able to turn that to your advantage."

Zeb bristled in front of her, apparently offended that the council would question her in the way they had. She imagined she should be equally upset, but it really didn't bother her. They did the best they could to make sense of the situation, exactly like she did. She patted her boss on the shoulder and smiled at the seated gnome. "That's good to know. Thank you so much for doing that. I deeply appreciate it."

"So," Vizidus said, "do we have anything more for Cali?" No one responded, and he nodded and looked at her. "Thank you for joining us and for being such a valuable friend to the citizens of New Orleans. The members of this council applaud your efforts."

Yeah, you're merely not willing to put your necks on the line to help with them. She sighed. *Quit being petty, Cali. You'd do the same if you were them.* "I appreciate that. Good night to you all."

She left without a backward glance and chose not to give away any of her dignity by saying something snippy. Fyre stared past her as she walked toward the stairs, his glare at the people in the room communicating all the things she held inside. When they reached the top, they portaled to her apartment. She patted him on his side. "People. Am I right?"

He gave his weird laugh. "Idiots, more like."

"It takes all kinds." She grinned.

The Draksa shook his head as he followed her into the bedroom. "It really doesn't. Next time, let me eat one of them. It'll send a message."

Cali pulled her jeans and shirt off and crawled under the covers, and he jumped up beside her and curled on top of the blanket. "So, which would you choose?"

He tilted his head to the side in consideration, then answered, "Malonne. He's one irritating Light Elf."

She laughed and burrowed deeper into the covers to think about what she might ask the Atlanteans when she kicked their asses next time.

CHAPTER TWENTY-THREE

Usha reclined on the comfortable couch in her office, leaned her head back, and stared at the ceiling. Even that had been repainted to try to remove the mental stain of it all after the violation of the space by Caliste Leblanc and her associates. Still, it hung in the air like a fine mist she would sometimes catch glittering in the corner of her vision.

Danna was talking. She had done so for several minutes, sharing details on the successful rollout of their highly addictive drugs to both the human and magical communities. The Empress had charged the gang leader with taking the city by whatever means necessary, and she was determined to do exactly that. If it required the deaths of a large portion of the population, well, they could import indentured workers instead of using drug-addicted people as their labor force.

Her ruler hadn't explained the reasons behind her desire for the city, of course. Things didn't work that way. It was merely, "Usha, I need it. Make it happen." Nothing more was required. And if she died in the process, the leader of the Atlantean gang in New Orleans would count herself lucky to have served. *Hopefully, Danna feels the same way about me. It seems like she does.* She tilted her head and looked at her second in command.

The woman had a glow about her lately. *It appears that increased authority is good for her.* She was in an even more perfectly cut suit than usual, a product of a new store she'd enthused about a week before. The gang took a smaller piece of the man's business in exchange for free clothes and services, and it appeared to work out quite well for her subordinate. It was a charcoal pinstripe that fell flawlessly over her crossed legs. Her shirt was the deepest black, and the tie atop it a shimmering blue.

Danna stopped speaking with a smile. "Why are you staring at me that way? I feel like I'm about to become lunch for a shark."

Usha laughed. "Well, I am hungry. But I was admiring your suit. Is it from Raynauld's?"

The other woman grinned widely. "Yes, isn't it fantastic? It's the best acquisition we've ever made, aside from our scientists." Her expression faltered somewhat. "Speaking of scientists, did you hear any more about the thing at the docks?"

It was a good choice of phrasing—the thing like the activity, or the thing like the giant sea monster that had attempted to wreak havoc in her city. They'd received notice a few days before the event that something big was in the works and a warning only minutes before the attack itself. The Empress had ordered them to stay out of the battle without any explanation and of course, she had obeyed. If given her own choice, she would have watched with glee while the creature eliminated her foes, then called for her people to destroy it when they were all dead. *There really isn't much point in ruling a broken city if other options are available.*

She nodded. "I communed with the Empress after the incident. A challenger to her rule has arisen in New Atlantis. The family is undergoing the trials now but apparently, has chosen not to limit themselves to the formal structure. Of course, they're working secretly enough to not appear to break the rules. The Kraken was developed by one of the Empress's scientists, a product of both magic and technology. That person was found dead and their research stolen in the days before the attack."

Danna nodded. "Hence the warning."

"Exactly. The upstarts apparently had sufficient riches, power, influence, friends, or all of the above to replicate his work and send the creature. Of course, they deny everything and until we can reliably make the dead speak, there is no way to be certain enough to halt the process."

"The process is archaic. We would be rid of Leblanc if not for that."

The leader shrugged. They'd had this discussion before and she didn't fault her subordinate for speaking her mind in private as long as she dutifully followed the rules. "It is what it is. Changing it would demand unanimity among the nine families, and such a thing is impossible." Since those ruling clans had set the laws down generations before, not once had there been enough agreement to change them. It would require a ruler who was willing to release a portion of their power and authority. The very things that allowed them to reach that position inevitably made them unwilling to part with the fruits of their labors.

Her second sighed, stood, and crossed to the small bar table that stood in the corner. She poured two glasses of rum, carried them back, and handed one over before she sank into the cushions again. Her boss nodded her thanks, and she gave a half-smile. "When you are the Empress, perhaps things will change."

Usha barked a laugh filled with frustration. "As if someone not of the families could be acknowledged as ruler. While it's possible within the laws, the odds are beyond small. No, I think I will have to be content with the role of the Empress's strong right hand. Fortunately, I can live with that, especially if it gives me the chance to make life difficult for the nine." Her hatred of the noble families was not because of anything they'd done to her but simply for their uselessness. When power was handed from one generation to the next, the worthiness of those who held that power decreased exponentially. *Such things should be earned, not given.*

Danna swirled the liquid in her glass with a worried look on her face. "Do you think we have more to fear from whoever sent the Kraken?"

"I don't think we have anything to fear from them or anyone else," she snapped before she softened her tone and continued. "I see two possibilities. First, they attempted to weaken the Empress in the eyes of the other eight by stealing the knowledge and then by putting it to use in a place she has claimed as her own. The creature's destination was certainly not randomly selected." Her second in command nodded. "Second, they are indifferent to the way the Empress is viewed and they actively wish to claim the city for themselves. If so, that should concern us but not instill fear." She wanted to drive the poor word choice home. It was imperative to keep the proper perspectives on everything and any challenge was simply something to overcome rather than be afraid of.

"And which of these options makes more sense to you?"

She drank the rest of the rum she'd been sipping and set the glass precariously on the padded arm of the couch. "I dislike both. The first is cowardly and the second a threat to our interests. If I was forced to choose, I would guess it was simply a play to weaken the image of the Empress because I can't imagine any of the nine summoning the initiative for anything more." She clapped her hands on her thighs and stood. "Fortunately, we don't need to choose. We'll plan for the worst-case and hope for the best. Let's head upstairs and see what's happening."

The office was heavily soundproofed, and the raucous music from the main part of the club hit her like a crashing wave as soon as she stepped outside. A local blues band was playing tonight and they laid down a serious groove. She crossed to the bar and took a seat, and her second slid onto the stool beside her. The bartender delivered a tumbler of dark rum to each of them with a stick of fresh fruit as a garnish. She lifted it and pulled a cube of papaya from the end while she surveyed the crowd.

Even without the money from all their illicit activities, the nightclub itself would probably make a profit. It was impossible, at this point, to separate the income streams and the books were entirely fabricated by a team of talented financial liars. But the audience loved the music and the clientele cut across gang lines. While not at all neutral territory since the Atlanteans owned it, the normal conflicts were left at the door. Any outbreaks of violence were squashed quickly and decisively. She watched without speaking for the duration of a song and let the hoarse words and the inspired jam session flow over her.

Usha bent her head to Danna and resumed their previous conversation. "If someone wanted to make a move on our interests in the city, they would have to come at us sideways and catch us by surprise. Otherwise, there's no way we'd fail to notice them infiltrating the streets. Of course, they might be able to portal a small army in, but we could fade and wait them out. No, it would have to be something else."

Her subordinate laughed. "There's enough room there for it to be almost anything."

She nodded. "True, which is why we'll need to be on our toes. Let's pull some of the weakest folks off the distribution team." They'd kept a much larger than normal presence around the drug trade to protect it from further Zatora attacks. *And those human bastards will get theirs soon enough.* "Position them throughout the city as lookouts. They must report anything out of the ordinary—cops, Zatoras, other magicals, and especially new Atlanteans in town. Oh, and the damned Leblanc girl and her friends. Choose three or four trusted people to rotate as a destination for the information. If something seems worthwhile, they can bring it to you."

"I could simply have the watchers contact me directly," Danna countered.

The leader shook her head. "You're too valuable to

waste on that task. Others of less competence can handle it. Besides, you need to sleep sometime, right?" She ran surveillance on her second in command from time to time because it was prudent to do so, the same way that Danna did with those most valuable to her and so on down the line. As near as she could tell, the other woman worked and slept and did very little else. *She reminds me of me on my way up.*

Her subordinate grinned. "Sleep is overrated."

The words summoned a wave of weariness that reminded her she was tired and had in fact been up for almost thirty-six hours dealing with the aftermath of the event that mangled the docks. She could use a rest herself. "You young people with so much energy. I'm off to bed."

The woman nodded. "I'll get the watchers out tonight."

"Excellent." She stood and put a hand on her shoulder. "You are a gem, and I don't know what I would do without you. I'm glad we're a team." Tears threatened, and she held them in check with an act of will. *I'm too tired and getting maudlin.* She turned and strode quickly to the office to portal home.

Danna Cudon watched her go and finished the chunks of fruit on her skewer before she drained the rest of her glass. She wasn't sure what the damn Kraken attack actually meant for them but was determined to find out. Things were best when they were predictable and controlled, at least where work was concerned.

She thought of the romantic interest in her life and

laughed at the name he'd given to Grisham. *Ozahl. Seriously. Who would believe that nonsense?* With a shake of her head, she summoned her magic and used it to push her tiredness away and to fill her muscles with energy. It would take hours to set up the network Usha wanted and hours more to speak in person with those who would report directly to her in spite of her superior's admonition against it.

Knowledge is power, but only if you have it before your competition does. And here in New Orleans, everyone is my competition.

CHAPTER TWENTY-FOUR

Cali gazed at the structure ahead of her with a frown. It was a 1601 commercial address, the second one she and Fyre had visited that day. The first had been a twelve-story building with offices above a coffee shop on the ground floor, and they'd agreed it was unlikely to be their target.

She'd tried the key on the entry doors anyway but it hadn't even come close to fitting. This address seemed more likely to be their destination. It was one of a cluster of two-story warehouse buildings and appeared vacant. Better still, a large padlock secured the front doors, one that might even be large enough to accommodate the over-sized key in her hand.

"Go on up," she said, and the Draksa elevated with strong beats of his expansive wings. He disappeared from view, although she could see the shimmer of his veil. They'd concluded that it was her other senses keeping track of him that allowed her to isolate the visual cue as well, which had been reassuring. She'd hate to think the telltale was visible to others.

He circled several times before he returned to land beside her. "It's all clear. There is not a soul around."

"Does that seem normal?"

His snout lowered and rose in a nod. "Yes. This seems like a very lightly traveled site. There aren't many tire tracks or footprints so maybe it's all abandoned."

That's a good sign maybe. Who the hell knows? She sighed. "Okay, the moment of truth." She strode forward and lifted the lock. The key slid in, and she had an instant of elation before it failed to turn. "Damn it to hell," she shouted at the top of her lungs, then yanked the key out. In a calmer voice, she observed, "The lock could be damaged. It wouldn't hurt to check inside."

"Sure, it's only breaking and entering, not one of the bigger crimes. Should I give Detective Barton a call now to save time?"

"Funny stuff, scale face. Don't quit your day job." She raised her hand and blasted the chain with a force bolt that shattered several links. "Oh, look, it's open."

The Draksa rolled his eyes, which was an impressive sight given their larger than expected size. Cali pulled the door open only far enough to slide inside and pushed down on the hope that threatened to fill her. Unfortunately, the interior was boring—an empty warehouse with debris and a few broken pallets scattered on the floor.

"Take a look around for me, will you?" The dragon lizard slithered away, and she cast about with every magical sense she had in search of anything that might be hidden or any clue at all. With a sigh, she announced, "There's nothing, right?"

"Exactly," he called in response.

With another sigh, she gestured toward the door and led the way out onto the street. She scowled at the lock. "Why even bother to secure the building if it's empty? Idiots." Logic wasn't welcome in her mind at the moment, and when it tried to suggest that valid reasons existed, she pushed the thought away.

She sat on the curb and held the key in front of her eyes. "Why do you suck so much? What are you for? Reveal your secrets, you stupid damned hunk of metal." It didn't seem to feel the need to obey her command and remained inert.

Fyre poked her with her nose. "Correct me if I'm wrong, but your parents were magicals, right?"

"Yes. So?"

"Well, if two magical people left a hidden message for another magical person, don't you think they might, maybe, just possibly, use magic?"

Cali lowered her head in amazement at her own stupidity. Her gaze focused on the ground, she said, "To be fair, both Emalia and likely Scoppic or Invel examined it magically."

"But they aren't you."

She moved her gaze to the object in her hands. *Don't crush my hopes, you bastard key. Not again.* Of course, she didn't know how to create the result she wanted or even where to start. An image of her parents floated into her mind, and she caught it and focused on it. She relaxed her hold on her power and willed for it to tell her something about the key.

Magic swelled within her, and the object glowed in her hand. She thought for a second she would receive a clue, but it faded into its scraped and dull sheen. Her spirit cracked at the sight, and she closed her eyes against the tears that had begun to form.

"Look again," Fyre said with a note of excitement in his voice.

She opened her eyes and saw a symbol in the circle made by the etched zero. She scrabbled for her phone and magnified the image to discover that it was a small compass, almost exactly like the one on the necklace she wore. Her mind whirled for a moment before an idea materialized. She snapped a picture of the design and dropped it into a reverse image search.

Compasses galore filled the results so she tried again and this time, limited the search with the numbers 1601. Only one result was returned, and she grinned. "They were clever people, my parents." It wasn't an address. Staring at her from the screen was the image of a mausoleum in Cemetery Number One, with no names or markings and its only notable feature a marble statue of an angel mounted over the door. It held a scroll with the etched numbers she sought. She turned to Fyre with a grin. "Damn, you're good."

"I know, right?"

She stood and brushed the seat of her jeans off. "Let's go get ready for this. We'll sneak in after dark."

Entering the cemetery was far easier this time than it had been on her previous visit. Cali used a force blast to propel herself over the wall when the coast was clear of witnesses and another to cushion her landing. Despite spending a good portion of the day searching the Internet and looking at all the pictures of the area she could find, she hadn't been able to pinpoint exactly where their target destination was located.

Fyre led the way since his heightened senses would provide an early warning if any predators—animals or humans—awaited them. The graveyard appeared to be deserted except for them, and it took only ten minutes of searching to find the mausoleum. She blew her breath out in relief. "I was sure this would be harder than it seemed. Let's see what my parents left for us."

But, after she'd circled the entire building with a growing sense of dismay, she was forced to acknowledge that nothing was ever easy, including legacies. She put her hands on her hips and looked at her companion. "So, there's no keyhole. Do you have any ideas?"

The Draksa sat and regarded the structure for some time without speaking. Finally, he stood and walked in a circle, looking outward. When she was about to yell at him for being an enigmatic jerk, he deigned to speak. "I can sense something magical going on here. Well, not actually magical. More like potentially magical. Does that make sense?"

She frowned. "Like a trap?"

He paced around one more time. "No, I don't think a trap. Usually, that has a more negative, doom-like feel. This is more like something's waiting."

"For a trigger. To explode."

The Draksa snorted, amused. "For a trigger, sure. To explode, probably not. I think your parents left you a puzzle."

Cali sighed and looked at the sky. "Seriously, you guys? I hope you're enjoying all this." She stalked forward to examine the mausoleum more closely. A rounded protrusion jutted from the center of the doors where she'd expect a lock to be, but it was seamless. She placed her hands on it and willed it to open as she allowed her power to flow out, but nothing happened. "Dang it. Of course that would be too easy. Okay, walk the path of where you feel the magic."

She watched as he paced an almost perfect diamond shape with the mausoleum on one point, two low headstones at the sides, and a tall marker with a spire at the far end. Her heart beat a little faster as she crossed to examine the markers. Each had unfamiliar names and birth and death years carved into the stone. They didn't seem to have anything in common, and by the conclusion of her second circuit, the anger had begun to hammer in her temples.

The emotion really didn't help so she forced herself to calm. Perhaps the puzzle was simple and meant to keep people without the key from entering. *So, if the key is the key, what could it mean?* She held it out and looked at it, hoping for a clue, but it gave her nothing.

Fyre stared at one of the low markers and interrupted her thoughts. "These stones each have a six, a zero, and two ones on them. Not together or in order, but present."

"I'll try pushing on them." She moved to each one and traced her fingers over them, but that didn't work either. Frustration was rising again, momentarily held back by his discovery, and she forced herself to focus through it. *I wonder if there's a spell to make myself stop freaking out so much. That would be helpful.* "Okay, let's put a little magic on the stones." She repeated what she'd done with the key, but while she felt a resonance from them, no revelation occurred. "What am I missing, Fyre?"

His voice was thoughtful. "How about you stand at the mausoleum and try the magic on the key again?" She shrugged and did as he asked. Again, the symbol appeared, and although she felt a stronger resonance, nothing in front of her changed. The Draksa, though, broke out into happy laughter. She whirled on him and snapped, "What?"

He raised an eyebrow. "You might want to take it down a notch. I'll wait." His superior tone was irritating but there was truth to his words.

"Okay. I'm good. Sorry."

"Turn and cast that spell again."

Cali obeyed, and as the resonance fluttered through her, a compass appeared on the ground. The north icon faced the stone to her left, even though that wasn't north. "Uh, okay." She moved toward it and the image vanished. "Damn. Wait. I got this." This time, she stuck the spell into a corner of her brain after she cast it so it wouldn't vanish when she did other things.

When she reached the stone, she knelt and whispered, "Please." She touched the first number one and outlined it with her finger. It started to glow. The compass beneath her—which now seemed to be part of the ground—spun to face the opposite way. She crossed to it and held her breath as she traced a six. The compass turned to the spire, and she hurried forward and caressed the zero.

It spun again and stopped with its point leading to the mausoleum. The first three numbers carved in the angel's scroll glowed. The image beneath her feet moved and coalesced into the center circle, which then floated toward the last digit. When it reached it, a click sounded and the protrusion on the door vanished to reveal a keyhole.

Cali stepped forward in a daze and inserted the key, which turned easily.

Fyre leaned into her and she looked at her friend and partner. "Are you ready for this?"

He nodded, and replied, "I think the more important question is whether you are ready for this."

She swallowed the lump that was stuck in her throat. "No. I don't think I could ever be. But that won't stop me. Let's do it." She pushed on the door and it swung open into the darkness.

CHAPTER TWENTY-FIVE

B ased on the size of the mausoleum, Cali had expected to find a small room on the opposite side of the barrier separating her from the secrets her parents had left. But, like so many things about her life lately, her expectations in the matter turned out to have very little to do with reality. Beyond the entrance, stairs led into the darkness, as wide as the double entry in the front wall of the structure.

She looked at Fyre. "Well. That's not at all like a horror movie. How about you go first and do a little recon? Let me know what you find."

He snorted at the joke. "How about not?"

"Aren't you supposed to be tough?" She sighed. "Fine, scaredy-Draksa, we'll go together." Her babble was merely a way to avoid heading into the dark. She wasn't sure if she was eager or terrified as it seemed to change from one millisecond to the next. With a sigh, she closed the main doors. While the moonlight outside had been bright enough to see well in, this descent required something more. She retrieved the small flashlight she'd shoved in the pocket of her jacket and flicked it on.

The stairs continued beyond the light's ability to illuminate them, although a hint of a wall showed at the bottom, possibly marking a turn of some kind. She released an unfocused version of the spell she'd used on the key and it returned a vague sense of magic around her. "Fyre, do you sense anything?"

There was a pause before he replied. "There is magic everywhere. It's too amorphous to identify specifics, although it's all around. In the walls, in the stairs, and in the doors, obviously."

"What do you think that means?"

"That you'd better be careful and keep an eye out since you'll go first."

She groaned. "Ha, ha, ha, funny dragon lizard." He'd made no move to step behind her, so she knew it was merely a taunt. "Let's go together." She stepped carefully down the first step, ready to retreat out of the building if something happened, but nothing did. By the third step, she no longer leaned back and by the fifth, she had increased her speed.

Seven turned out to be an unlucky number. When her foot settled on that one, it collapsed into a pit and took steps eight, nine, and ten along with it. She screamed, flailed, and managed to catch the lip of the hole for an instant before she lost her grasp and fell. Something slapped her in the face, and she instinctively caught hold of it. She hung from Fyre's tail as she gasped for breath and hoped her heart wouldn't explode.

When she regained her senses, she asked softly, "Will you pull me up or must I climb?"

"Climb." He sounded like he was under strain. Cali pulled herself up, clutching around his tail until her arms and shoulders screamed in pain, and finally made it to solid ground. She collapsed beside him and saw that his claws had dug into the stone of the stairs. "Damn. Thanks. I guess I panicked. I probably could have used force magic to come up."

He moved beside her and gave a short laugh. "Maybe not. Take a look."

She sat and stretched on her stomach to gaze into the pit. At the bottom, her flashlight illuminated a series of wicked spikes that she estimated at four feet tall—all iron and barbed. *And, hell, probably rusty and poisoned too.* "Geez. What the what, Mom and Dad?"

Fyre's snout moved side to side. "Yeah. This is more than I thought we would find."

"Right? I thought some gifts, maybe a codebook so we could read the journal, and possibly a treasure horde. But evil death pits hadn't really entered my mental picture."

"It would probably be good to consider this enemy territory until we discover what's going on."

Cali nodded in agreement. "Yeah." She remembered the opening scene of *Raiders of the Lost Ark* with a twist in her stomach. Pushing that thought aside, she sent a command to her bracelets to transform them into sticks, then clapped the ends together and willed them to join into a jo staff. "Okay, so…you jump over the pit and make sure the other side is solid since you can fly. I'll come after you and use this to test farther ahead."

He cleared the opening with ease and she followed with a little more effort. They resumed their descent while she prodded each step before them with the stick. Privately, she had already decided that whoever had created the trap wasn't likely to repeat themselves but then she second-guessed that idea. *Wouldn't it be more clever to do it again?* She shut that train of thought down before it could get her too twisted up.

The next defense turned out to be a rain of spikes that traveled with the force of arrows from the ceiling above. She'd triggered it with her staff so they were safely out of the barrage. The metal projectiles clanged as they bounced down the stairs ahead of them and into the wall she'd seen earlier. Cali sighed. "Dang, they're really serious about the security stuff, aren't they?"

"I wonder what's down here that needs so much protection."

"I've wondered the same thing. Do you think it's actually a treasure of some kind? Honestly, what else warrants these kinds of safeguards?"

He shook his head. "I don't know. But whatever it is, it was so important to hide it that they went underground with all the magical challenges that involves. We're probably surrounded by mud and water at this point."

Codebook. My kingdom for a codebook. "Well, there's only one way to find out. Let's keep moving." They navigated a couple more physical traps before they reached their first magical one. Fyre sensed it as they approached, which was the only thing that kept her from accidentally triggering it. Tripwires were set at ankle, knee, and chest heights and obscured from view by a veil. Only after he'd assured her they existed was she able to detect the incredibly subtle shimmer of the illusion. She could see no way through them and no obvious means to deactivate them.

She sighed. "We'll have to portal to the other side."

"That's a bad idea," the Draksa countered. "Portal blockers exist and maybe even redirectors. Plus, it's always dangerous to teleport somewhere you haven't been."

"I'm only going over there." She pointed. "I can see it from here. There's no risk."

"There's always a risk."

"Do you have a better idea?"

He paused for a second before answering. "No."

Cali nodded decisively. "So. Shut up, then." She gestured with her arms and summoned a portal to connect the place where she stood to a position several feet away on the other side of the wires. Ignoring the voice that told her how stupid the plan was, she rolled her neck, took a deep breath, and thrust through.

She landed cleanly where she wanted to be and waved at Fyre. He followed her with a grumble and she let the rift fall. They continued until finally, they reached a door. It was metal, solid, and big enough for two people to enter simultaneously. A shelf protruded beside it, and the top surface was a handprint.

The Draksa rose on his hind legs to examine it, then lowered himself again. "That's subtle. I think—and don't quote me on this because I might be wrong—you're supposed to put your hand in there."

"When did you become such a cynic?"

"You must have rubbed off on me."

"Ooh, good one. So, what do you think will happen

when I do it?"

"Only awesome things, I'm sure."

"Seriously, lighten up, dude." She bumped him with her leg. He grumbled again and didn't reply. *Maybe the constant danger is getting to him. It's sure as hell getting to me.* She considered simply walking away, but it was her parents who had set her on the path that brought her there, as convoluted as it was, and that required her to see it through to the end.

She placed her hand in the receptacle. A faint glow emanated from it, then grew in intensity. Finally, a sharp stab lanced into her index finger and she pulled it back with a yelp to see a drop of blood. The needle descended into the small hole it had come from. Cali frowned and muttered, "Great. Now I need to find out when my last tetanus shot was."

Fyre sounded more like himself when he replied, "Oh, I don't know. You having lockjaw might be nice. Let it slide."

The door shifted sideways to provide them access to the room beyond. Lights flickered on overhead with a slight hum and their fluorescent bulbs cast everything in a slightly otherworldly harsh light. She walked through the opening with Fyre at her side.

The first thing she noticed was the mosaic on the floor. It was a representation of the compass symbol she'd seen on the key and that she wore around her neck but done in tile and precious stones. The room was square, and the compass points touched the middle of each side. The door they'd come through was indicated by the southern point. She stood on the image and for a moment and thought it might cause a reaction, but nothing happened.

The next thing to catch her eye was the opposite wall. It was about twenty feet long and most of it was covered with pictures, newspaper clippings, printouts, colored strings, pins, and handwritten notes. She walked toward it with a complete lack of understanding. *Why would my parents have led me here? Whose place is this? Some kind of police zone?* When she drew closer, she saw that all the items related to the city's gangs, primarily the magical ones although images of Zatora figures were present as well. She recognized a younger Rion Grisham in one of the photos and scowled.

"Cali, look here," Fyre said, and she turned to the wall indicated by the west pointer. It had a large desk full of notebooks and papers. She picked up the first one she came to and growled in frustration.

"It's the same damn code. I recognize it but I can't read it. Where the hell did they get all this?" She sifted through the items on the dented metal surface but found nothing that provided any ideas at all about what was going on. Pressure had begun to build in her brain and a small voice screamed about how unfair it was that the resolution of one mystery had led to more.

Finally, she turned and walked the axis of the room to reach the last wall. It was entirely covered by lockers several feet taller than her. They looked like the versions found in a gym, about twice as wide as the ones she'd used in school back in the day. Ten stood in a row, and she realized that she was absolutely afraid to open them. Still, not doing so could never be an option. With a deep breath, she pulled on the first handle.

CHAPTER TWENTY-SIX

"And that's when I found them," Cali exclaimed and almost bounced in her seat due to a complete inability to contain herself. "I couldn't believe it."

Tanyith and Zeb both performed the calm down gesture this time, but she was unable to obey. The discoveries she'd made in what she now thought of as her parents' secret lair were too exciting. After looking through it all once, she'd portaled directly to the tavern and apologized to Zeb for calling off. Waiting for the last customers to leave had been difficult but finally, everyone was gone except the three of them and Fyre, and she'd launched into the tale.

"Take a breath," the man said, "then tell us what you found. Honestly, you are the most annoying storyteller ever." The Draksa snorted his agreement from behind the bar. Her boss pushed a soft cider into her hands, and she drank greedily before she resumed her description of the evening.

"So, the first two lockers had black uniform-like outfits

in them—jacket, shirt, pants, and boots. Clearly, one belonged to my mother and one to my father because one was my size and I'm about her size, and the other was bigger. They also had the compass symbol on them in several places but hidden under Velcro patches. They looked brand-new."

Tanyith replied, "That's unexpected. What else did you find?"

"The third and fourth lockers were filled with shelves holding all kinds of different things. Healing and energy potions. Electronic equipment I didn't recognize. Big zip ties like the police use. And a couple of black motorcycle helmets with tinted faceplates."

Zeb shook his head. "This gets weirder and weirder. We need to check those potions before you even think about using them, though."

Cali nodded. "I can take you both there later if you want to go. I made sure I knew the place well enough to portal back."

"Field trip," Tanyith quipped. "Nice. How about tomorrow morning?"

The dwarf shrugged but she could tell he was intrigued. "That sounds good."

"Can I continue now? Are you done talking? Good." She hadn't even reached the best part yet. "The fifth and sixth lockers held pieces of metal similar to the sword fragment they left me. Some seemed smaller like they might be from knives based on the size of the etchings in them."

The man frowned. "So do you think your parents were actively collecting those things?"

"Totally, yes. It explains so much if they were. Maybe

they got in someone's way while they were doing it." The realization hit her in the face like a roundhouse punch, and her voice became a low growl. "Maybe they got in the way of the Atlantean gang. We know they have one of the sword pieces." She turned fiery eyes to him. "Was the fragment there when you were part of them?"

"No. I would have known if it was. It's possible that it could have arrived toward the end, when I was already being ignored and pushed out, but we definitely didn't have it for most of my time there."

She caught the reins of her suspicion and pulled back hard. "Okay. That makes sense. Sorry." He nodded and she returned to relating what she'd found. "Seven had only a large sheath for a sword. It had etchings similar to the ones on the blade they left me, but not the same. I checked the picture against it and they didn't match."

"Eight held what I can only call spy stuff. Fancy binoculars, what looked like little listening devices and receivers, and a variety of other things I couldn't even make a guess at."

Tanyith drummed his fingers on the bar. "What the hell were your parents up to? This sounds like much more than merely collecting artifact pieces."

Cali sighed at the interruption. "I agree with you, but I have absolutely no idea. After I saw the lockers, I deduced that everything on the wall must have been about tracking the fragments. Maybe it wasn't? Maybe they had more than one thing they were working on? I honestly don't know."

"Yeah. There are a ton of questions in need of answers at this point, that's for sure."

"Wait until you hear about the last two lockers." This

was the part she couldn't wrap her mind around at all. She had the feeling it would strike at some inopportune moment and overwhelm her to the point of shut-down but so far, she was doing okay. "The ninth one was empty except for a nameplate on the shelf separating the tall bottom section from the top. Etched into it was *Caliste Leblanc.*"

Zeb's eyes widened. "So, they assumed you would join them when you were old enough, I guess?"

She shrugged. "That was my thought too. It seems like the most likely explanation, doesn't it?"

Tanyith nodded. "It does. What about the last one?"

"Another empty locker. Another nameplate, identical to the first except for what was engraved on it." They stared at her, waiting, while she mastered herself enough to speak. "*Atreo Leblanc.*" She paused, then forced herself to say it. "It appears I have a brother."

It had taken her almost a quarter of an hour to pull herself together after saying the words out loud. She didn't know where the certainty that the last nameplate was her sibling came from, but when she saw it, she simply knew in her blood and bones and soul and mind. Cali stared at herself in the mirror of the tavern's ladies' room and deeply troubled eyes looked back. She choked out a single laugh. *Yeah, you and me both, sister. You look how I feel.*

She returned to the bar to find the men deep in conversation and slid onto the stool without interrupting. Tanyith said, "It shouldn't be that hard to get to the bottom of it. There have to be records."

Zeb shook his head. "If there are, they're probably in New Atlantis."

"I could ask Kendra."

"So it's Kendra, is it?" she interjected. "What will you ask her? Out on a date?" Without her normal good humor behind it, the jest fell flat.

"To look into you and your parents and see if there's any information to be had on this mysterious name in the locker."

Her boss folded his arms, clearly against the idea. "Cali needs less attention from the police, not more. I like the detective but we can't afford to trust her. Not with this. No, we'll have to do that work ourselves."

Tanyith shrugged and looked at her. "What do you think?"

"I'll go with Zeb on this one. I'd prefer to see what we can find on our own before we take it beyond the four of us." From his place behind the bar, Fyre snorted in approval of being included. "Well, five, since I'll ask Emalia. I can't imagine that she would have held this back from me, though."

"She's concealed other important things." The frown on her partner's face showed his reluctance to say anything that could be seen as negative about her great aunt.

"True. But she wasn't really a part of their lives until they came here, so whatever made this a secret might have been something that happened before. Either way, we'll see." She shook her head. "I can't imagine my parents leaving their child behind for any reason."

Zeb's voice was gruff. "I can think of one. He's no longer alive."

Cali knew why he'd made the blunt statement. The dwarf was a consistent proponent of the Band-Aid approach—yank it off fast and make it hurt because drawing it out would cause it to hurt so much more. She nodded. "It's possible. But even then, I have to know."

"Of course you do. And we have to help you find out."

Tanyith sighed. "Okay, no Barton. Maybe Emalia will have something. I can check the library to see if there are any genealogies. It's a super-long shot but sometimes, the Hail Mary pass gets caught, right?"

The dwarf snorted. "Not by this year's team."

She raised a hand. "We are not shifting from my potentially long-lost brother to talking about the Saints. No way, no how." Her tension eased as they all laughed together but inside, she still felt wobbly like the ground beneath her was no longer as solid as it had been. She took a deep breath to center herself, then turned to face Tanyith. "So, I hear you have time on your hands now and then. How about I help you with your investigation and you try to find out what was going on with my parents? Maybe if I look into yours and you look into mine, fresh eyes will reveal things we're too close to see."

He shrugged. "I couldn't do much worse on my side of the equation. Aiden has apparently vanished from the face of the Earth and the more I hear about this Harry guy, the more I hope it isn't him."

Cali nodded. "And the more I try to understand what my parents were up to, the more I get upset that they never told me. Maybe some distance will help us both."

"That sounds like a good arrangement," Zeb agreed. "You should do it. However, you should do it somewhere else. I need to get some rest if we're going to visit your new discovery tomorrow morning."

"You sleep?" She laughed. "I was sure you spent all your time here, walking around and talking to yourself."

He merely shook his head. "Go. Now. Both of you."

She was smiling as she headed to the basement to portal home, but the questions would not stop banging around her head. *Why didn't my parents tell me about Atreo, and where is he now?*

CHAPTER TWENTY-SEVEN

They'd explored every corner and crevice of her parents' secret lair but discovered nothing more than what she'd found before. When the others had left, she'd tried the uniform on and discovered that it fit almost perfectly. It was lightweight but conveyed a sense of solidness. The material was unfamiliar, and she intended to ask Nylotte to look at it as soon as she could.

After that, she'd gone to speak with Emalia, who was as stunned as she had been at the discovery of the bunker and her presumed brother. That was her great aunt's phrase—presumed brother. Cali had no doubts. She pressed the older woman a little but had no sense of deception. *Which is good. If I discovered she was lying to me, I don't know what I'd do. Probably fall to pieces.*

She needed to understand what her parents had been up to. Clearly, they had a passion, a mission, a crusade—something to explain all the weird things she'd found. If it was in her power to continue it, and if it was worthy of being continued—which it was, of course, because they had thought it was worth it—she would give it her all. The frustration at not knowing became almost overwhelming at times, and she'd spent considerable time that day with her arms wrapped around Frye while she tried to blank her mind. He seemed to know what she needed and hadn't strayed more than a couple of feet from her.

The ritual of serving the tavern's Thursday night crowd took her mind off her bigger concerns and grounded her in the everyday annoyance of people whose belief in their own intelligence grew with every glass or bottle they emptied. Tonight, she was all about being involved with them and traded insults and arguments with all takers. Zeb's watchful eye lingered on her but he didn't tell her to stop so she indulged herself.

By the time the evening was winding down, she felt more like herself than she had since the discovery of the key's hidden secret. About two dozen people remained in the common room when the front door banged open and Tanyith rushed in, followed by Detective Barton. Her first inclination was to rush over and tease them for being together, but the expressions on their faces stopped her. He looked as angry as she'd ever seen him, and the woman wore what she thought of as her cop face—hard, unyielding, suspicious, and intense.

She headed to the bar, where they were already speaking to Zeb. As she moved into earshot, the detective's words sent a chill through her. "Yes, another gang or group or something."

Cali reached them and interrupted. "What's going on?"

Tanyith said, "We've had warning of an imminent attack—within the hour."

Adrenaline surged through her. "On us? Here?"

Barton shook her head. "On the Zatoras."

She frowned. "Do we care about that now?"

The detective sighed. "Yeah, we do, for two reasons. First, it's a new player and we don't know what they're doing or why they're doing it. We don't even have a guess. Second, they intend to do it in public."

"What? Why?" she blurted. "How do you know?" Panic rocketed through her and Fyre stood with a growl behind the bar, apparently reacting to her emotional state. She pushed the emotion down but couldn't banish it.

"An informant near the Atlantean gang. A signal went up to pull all their people off the streets, and he was able to find out why. The local leader has a boss in New Atlantis, and word came down that another group from there will make a move here tonight. The group that's already in town was expressly forbidden to get involved. It's apparently something about the way politics works for them. Frankly, it sounds stupid." *You're preaching to the choir on that one, sister.* "But here's the worst part. He said they're the ones who sent the giant octopus."

Her mouth corrected, "Kraken," without instruction from her brain as she considered the possibilities. She didn't much care if a group of criminals attacked another one as long as they kept it between themselves. *Maybe that makes me a bad person. If so, I'll wear that.* But if the public was at risk, they had a responsibility to act. "Okay. If we have to choose a side, it's against the bastards who sent a freaking monster to destroy the city. What's the plan?"

"The police are going to do what they can," Tanyith

answered, "but there's no way they will be able to watch everywhere. We need to fill the gaps."

Barton nodded. "I've already put the word out and we're spinning up. But we can't bring in the National Guard. It would cause a complete panic. So it'll be patrol, SWAT, and the rest of us positioned on the streets. But the Zatora gang holds considerable territory, and we don't have the numbers to cover it all. We need help."

"I'll contact the council," Zeb said. "They'll want to secure their neighborhoods first but should be able to spread out from there." He headed to the basement—apparently, he wanted to keep his secrets secret from the tavern's clientele.

Cali turned to the Draksa. "It's time to get up top and look for trouble. If you find it, let me know." She'd feel his emotion through the connection between them and she could always tell what direction he was in from wherever she was. Neither of them fully understood the reasons for this but accepted it happily. Tanyith opened the door for him, and he dashed through it.

The detective nodded. "I have to go. Call me if you need help. Stay safe and thank you."

Honesty resonated in her words, so Cali skipped the sarcastic response she'd normally have made and stuck with a gentle tease, instead. "You stay safe, Detective." Barton grinned like she'd heard the unsaid, "Because your boyfriend here would miss you," and headed out the door.

Tanyith leaned against the bar across from her. "So. This sucks."

"Yeah. It really does. When this is all said and done, we

need to get a better understanding of what the hell is going on in New Atlantis."

"And we thought the local gang was trouble. Little did we know."

She laughed. "Right?" Her instincts—or her anxiety—prodded her to move. "You know, we're not of any use in here. I'll rush home and snag what I need. I can meet you here in ten, then let's go hunting. Does that sound good?"

"Perfect." With scant regard for the public area he was in, he created a portal and vanished.

Quickly, she turned to the tavern's crowd. "Listen up, people. There's trouble on the streets tonight. If you're interested in helping your city and sober enough to manage it, get out there and protect the innocent citizens and tourists who might be caught in it. If you're not, find someplace safe to hunker down." She summoned her own portal and plunged through it to her apartment.

Cali raced through her home to retrieve her full supply of healing and energy potions—two of each—and don the jacket Nylotte had given her. She had her bracelets and the charm necklace, as always. The idea of wearing the uniform she'd found in the lair had crossed her mind, but she'd rejected it since it was still untested and an unknown. *But there is something there I might be able to use. I'm an idiot for not taking them sooner.* She created another portal and hurried through into the center of the lair. The lights recognized her presence and kicked on as she ran to the lockers, pulled the zip ties out, and jammed them through two of her belt loops to keep her hands free. They were more than long enough to stay in place.

Another portal landed her in the tavern basement. Zeb

stood inside his secret room, talking to the air. She stared for a moment, wondered what magic he used or if he'd finally lost his mind, then turned and raced up the stairs. Tanyith waited at the top, wearing his Drow-provided jacket and a belt with sheaths for his sai. At the sight of her approach, he strode to the door and they exited together.

"Where to?" he asked.

She'd considered that question on the way over and had an answer ready. "We should move toward Jackson Square. It would be an unfortunate place for a battle, with Cafe du Monde right there plus all the bars and shops on Decatur, but if it's a public place they're after, that's my best bet."

"Okay, that's a good plan. Let's move."

Cali chose basically the opposite route she would have taken at any other time. Normally, she tried to avoid the most heavily trafficked areas. Tonight, they needed to be among the people so they could react to trouble. It took a few blocks before the crowds began to thicken. Tourists with huge containers of one drink or another wandered through the streets and generally had a good time. Sometimes, she thought they were ridiculous but on this occasion, she saw them simply as folks trying to fill a few hours with pleasure and freedom. The idea that jerks from out of town—way out of town—decided it was okay to interfere with that pursuit filled her with righteous anger.

She growled to release a little of the emotion. "I'm ready to bust heads. How about you?"

Tanyith nodded in her peripheral vision. "I'd rather it was the Zatoras or the Atlantean gang, myself, but I guess sometimes, life doesn't work out the way you want."

Her snort contained a thread of grim humor. "Maybe

Grisham will be so thankful he'll agree to leave town." Tanyith laughed, but a wave of anger from Fyre distracted her. She'd constantly tracked his location, and he was a block ahead and another toward the river. "Fyre's found something. It's time to make a deposit in the Karma bank." She accelerated into a run to find out what had upset the Draksa.

CHAPTER TWENTY-EIGHT

They rounded the corner with Cali a step ahead of Tanyith and they both froze for a moment when they immediately located what they had hoped to not find. People fled in panic from a battle that involved individuals with guns on one side and blasts of magic on the other. As one, they closed at a run while she cataloged the situation.

There are five on the left. They are human so probably Zatora with pistols. The three on the right are magicals using shadow and fire. Already, a parked car one of the humans had hidden behind was aflame, and she hoped the gangster would have the sense to move away from it before it exploded.

She sent a message to Fyre and told him to ice the vehicle before she turned her attention to the newcomers who launched a steady fusillade of magic at the gang members. They wore dark-blue clothes, similar enough to be a uniform but with notable differences. The tight pants and high boots were all the same, but one wore a coat that buttoned up to her neck, another displayed a different style jacket open over a tunic of some kind, and the third wore a top that looked like a heavy sweatshirt. Their positioning was effective as they used nearby cars as protection against the incoming bullets, and each carried an oval shield of their chosen form of magic in one hand and used the other to direct magical attacks at their opponents.

The Draksa whipped in front of her in response to her instruction and both the slight shimmer and her sense of his location confirmed he was there. A long stream of frost emerged to coat the car. One of the magicals reacted instantly and fired a shadow blast at the source. He flipped to avoid it and turned toward the one who had attacked him.

Cali yelled, "I'm on the right one," and Tanyith focused on the middle by default.

"Quit shooting and get the hell out of here," she shouted at the humans, then had to focus on defense as a fire blast streaked toward her and expanded with each foot it traveled. She launched herself upward and the cone tracked her, which forced her to conjure a shield to intercept it. Hers wasn't as good as Nylotte's had been, but it had improved enough to prevent her from being cooked. She landed behind the line of enemies, but only her target turned to her. The others were fully engaged with her allies.

Fyre's foe blasted him and hurled him sideways to crash onto the roof of a nearby building. Red rage blinded her and the magic erupted from her in a force blast that lifted the woman who'd targeted him from her feet and thrust her face-first into the car she had hidden behind. She crumpled, clearly unconscious.

Cali's original adversary used the moment of distraction to release another wash of flame at her, but she blocked it easily with her shield. He maintained the spell and effectively prevented her from releasing a counterattack. She raced to her right and a position that would require him to stop the attack or immolate his own ally.

Tanyith ruined that plan by eliminating the third of the New Atlanteans. Her partner had summoned shields on both hands and pushed into hand-to-hand distance to deliver a flurry of blows to the man. He finished it with an uppercut that lifted him onto his toes and a spinning back kick that catapulted him into the flames.

The disruption allowed her to drop her shield, and she delivered air punches that landed as force impacts on her opponent's ribs and head. She continued the battering until he was down, unmoving, and finally forced herself to stop. "Tanyith, check them and see if you can find anything useful. Where they came from. What they're up to. That junk." She turned without waiting for an answer and flung herself up to the roof where the Draksa had vanished.

Fyre lay under a piece of bulky equipment that appeared to have toppled onto him when he struck it. She raced over and pushed on it, but it was too heavy. With a scream that released all the pent frustration inside her, she pounded it with all the magical force she could muster and it shifted off her partner. She knelt beside him and put a hand on his side. "Are you okay, buddy?"

He snorted. "Those jerks burned a year's worth of luck. There is a one in a thousand chance of that falling on me."

She laughed. "So get up then."

The Draksa pushed himself to his feet and wobbled

slightly. "I'll need a little more time to heal. It took all the power I had to keep from being crushed."

"We'll head to the Square. Join us when you can."

He sat to wait for his flesh to knit and his strength to return, and she jumped to the ground, using her magic to break her fall. Tanyith strode over to her. "Nothing. Not a damn thing. They're here to fight and that's all, apparently."

Frustrated, she shook her head. "Well, let's give them what they came for."

They reached Jackson Square without any further encounters, although she heard a noise in the distance that sounded like fighting. Everything was strangely normal. Even though it was on the line between evening and night, an abundant number of tourists still wandered around. The usual assortment of buskers who frequented the area were there as well, and she saw Dasante first. She ran to him and interrupted his magical patter by stepping in front of his customers.

"Cal, what the hell?" He sounded far more surprised than upset.

"You have to go—now. Pack it up and go. There's trouble coming. Spread the word." Tanyith was already doing exactly that and moved quickly from person to person to advise them to get off the streets.

It was a sign of his trust in her that Dasante didn't argue and instead, began to gather his belongings. She turned and yelled, "Everyone clear the square. Now!" She growled in frustration as the people ignored her—or worse, laughed at her. Before she could respond, however, Fyre flew overhead and when he roared and spat frost magic, they hastily reconsidered. Screaming and running ensued, and all she could do was laugh at the sight. *See, you should have listened to me.* The Draksa was in his element as he alternately swooped low to make people move faster and soared high to make sure they could all see him.

She sent him appreciation and he responded with amusement. Ten minutes later, the area was clear and Tanyith, Cali, and Fyre stood in the center and took a moment to soak in the quiet. She'd never seen the square like this and honestly never wanted to again. It was as if the life had suddenly drained from it, leaving it physically and spiritually empty.

The respite lasted all of five minutes before the sounds of approaching voices from both sides alerted them to trouble on the way. Fyre launched into the air and vanished behind his veil, and his two teammates held a position in the center of the space, waiting to see what would happen. The Zatoras appeared from one corner, a pack of ten angry-looking humans with weapons in their hands and who bellowed insults in all directions. A group of New Atlanteans in their blue outfits emerged from around another corner. They numbered fewer than the gang members, but they moved with almost military position and obviously checked for enemies in all directions as they marched forward.

Cali caught Tanyith's shirt and pulled him into hiding behind a nearby hedge. "That's too many for us to handle on our own, even with Fyre."

He nodded. "We'll have to let them engage and step in once the numbers are down."

"I hate that."

"Yeah, me too. But I'm not really in a place where a noble, sacrificial death works for me at the moment."

She laughed. "Well said. And I can't die without knowing what the deal is with everything my parents left for me."

They fell silent as the two groups came to a stop facing each other, about thirty feet away near the entrance to the Cathedral. One of the New Atlanteans, a tall man with dark hair, took a step ahead of his teammates and shouted across the distance that separated them. "Lay down your weapons and you'll get a quick death."

The Zatora soldiers all laughed at him. A spokeswoman stepped forward with long wavy black hair, a leather jacket, and a shining silver pistol held in her hand. "Do you honestly think you can come into our city and say what's what? You'd best step back to where you came from."

"We can't do that."

"Then I guess we have a problem."

Her words were the catalyst for the chaos to begin. The Zatoras scattered, which allowed some of them to survive the roiling wall of flame that surged hungrily toward them. Gunshots rang out amidst the screams and a couple of the New Atlanteans fell before the others halted their attack and summoned shields. The human forces attacked and the magicals fired targeted assaults. Shadow and force magic reached out for individuals and lightning cascaded to catch two who had huddled too close together.

After the initial barrage, the gang members became a

little smarter and began to coordinate their fire, a strategy that eliminated two more of their enemies. The numbers were about even, and Cali put her hand on Tanyith's shoulder, ready to dart out and join the battle. Before she could move, however, a wave of agitation came from Fyre and suddenly, another dozen New Atlanteans appeared. She imagined this was how non-magicals felt when magicals did things that seemed impossible. One minute, they weren't there and the next, they were. Their veil had been so perfect that even the Draksa hadn't detected them.

The new arrivals annihilated the remaining Zatora soldiers in an instant as fire, force, and shadow overwhelmed any possibility of defense or retaliation. The survivors among the invaders gathered in a circle, presumably to talk.

"What the hell do we do now?" she whispered,

Tanyith's voice held the fear she felt. "Back away slowly and find another place to fight. We can't face that many."

She shook her head barely an inch to each side. "If we move, they'll see us." She felt a poke from Fyre but not as intense as before. "Wait. Something's happening." She heard footsteps coming from Decatur and pulled Tanyith with her to the other side of their cover so they wouldn't be seen from that direction either.

A group of Zatora soldiers, harder-looking than those who had first engaged the raiders, marched together toward the New Atlanteans. The main rank in the rear consisted of a dozen or so people arranged in three rows, and three individuals walked before them. Everyone was clad in what looked like body armor. A step back from and flanking the lead person were the two who had followed her before. In front of them was Grisham's lieutenant, the smaller man who had stood closer to the bar when they'd visited the Drunken Dragons.

"Hey, scumbags," he shouted. "You've had your fun. This is your chance to leave. If you don't, we will hunt and kill every last one of you. And we're gonna take our time with it."

One of the New Atlantean reinforcements stepped ahead of the others and his people fanned out behind him in a line. "Ah, Grisham's pet. I've looked forward to meeting you. We won't go anywhere."

The man shook his head. He was visually unimpressive and in his black tactical outfit, he looked even smaller than he had before. His hair was brown, his eyes were dull, and he radiated a sense of palpable boredom. But his smile carried a wicked edge that made it seem like he possessed a depth beyond what was visible at the moment.

His next words reinforced that impression. "Then you die."

CHAPTER TWENTY-NINE

Magic exploded out of the New Atlantean contingent, aimed at the man and the force arrayed behind him. With a negligent wave, he shielded all of them, and when the attack stopped, not a single Zatora had been hurt.

"What the actual hell is up with this dude?" Cali whispered.

The humans and their magical leader boiled toward their adversaries with a loud chorus of shouts. Pistols barked, and the invaders' formation changed as those in the front summoned shields and those behind them lofted fireballs above their protectors. The Zatora mage intercepted their attacks with blasts of ice, which resulted in a cold rain that spattered everyone, including her and Tanyith. The man was a dervish and defended against assaults from half the assembled enemies on his own.

"He won't be able to keep that up for long," her partner muttered. "There's no way."

She had to agree and had no idea what his strategy was,

other than buying time. *For what? A magical monster of their own? That would be a really bad sign if suddenly, New Orleans was ground zero for Kaiju battles.* The answer became apparent when the duo closest to him angled out to each side and drew weapons that had hung from straps around their necks, hidden behind their backs.

Each carried an assault rifle—she didn't know what kind, but they looked like what the military used. The ammunition magazines were wrapped in a stripe of blue tape, which seemed odd. They waited for the next round of fireballs and the moment when everyone's eyes would track them—except for Cali, who couldn't tear her gaze from the weapons. Their muzzles flashed and New Atlanteans fell. Four of them were down before they realized what was happening. The rest repositioned and those at the edges took a step back to bring the shields in line with the weapons.

Well, that's that, she thought and tensed, ready to race out and join the fray. She had already decided to use the same tactic and hunt around the fringes. Before she could act, the weapons discharged once again. She was possibly only slightly less surprised than the targets when the next round of bullets punched through their magical shields without stopping and killed the defenders. Tanyith hitched a breath. "Holy hell. They are using anti-magic bullets. They shouldn't have those."

Cali growled with quiet rage. "And if they did, they damn well should have brought them to use against the bloody octopus. Bastards." The rare ammunition changed the equation considerably. She didn't have anything to protect herself with against the rounds, so exposing herself to the battle now would be beyond stupid. Instead, she sent a message to Fyre and told him to fly higher for fear the anti-magic ammo might negate the innate protection he had that allowed him to shrug injuries off.

The Zatoras calmly obliterated the enemy with a combination of bullets, blades, and sweeping magical attacks by their leader that struck with lethal intensity. Whoever he was, he was far more than the persona he presented. *Which has to be a deliberate choice. Damn Grisham. He's a clever bastard to have his own personal mage in hiding.*

Fyre sent a warning from above and she felt him surge eastward, following Decatur. The Zatoras were reorganizing over the bodies of their enemies and the leader seemingly broke them into groups to send in different directions on a hunt for more of the invaders. She shook her head in dismay. *Something has to be done about all this. I don't know what it is, but something.* She grabbed Tanyith by the shoulder and said, "Follow me," then ran to the exit of the Square farthest from the Zatoras.

A lack of shouts in response told her they'd made their escape cleanly—or that the human forces had decided not to pursue them. *It was arrogant of the New Atlanteans to come in matching uniforms. That gave their enemies clear targets. I'm sure they won't make that mistake again.* A trickle of despair moved through her when she realized there would almost certainly be another attack. *And another, and another until someone stops them at the source.*

She put that future concern out of her mind and accelerated into a sprint as she sensed the emotions she associated with combat coming from Fyre. The creature was a born warrior based on the surging confidence and pleasure she felt from him whenever he fought. They arrived at the scene to find the Draksa in a complicated series of airborne maneuvers to distract five blue-uniformed New Atlanteans from the cringing and wailing citizens they'd trapped in an open-air restaurant.

With a shouted curse, one of them turned to target the huddled crowd and was instantly battered by a force bolt from her and a shadow bolt from Tanyith. The double attack hurled the man six feet away to land hard on his back on the pavement. The remaining four spun to face them. They broke in separate directions, him to the left and she to the right, and summoned shields to protect themselves from the shadow attacks that assailed them. The impact of the bolts on her magical protection pulled at her power, an indication that this group was stronger than many of the others she'd faced.

But not as strong as we are. While the enemies were distracted by them, Fyre swooped in, breathed frost on one, and scraped another with his claws. He didn't manage to fully ice the first, however, and the man broke free and fired a shadow attack at the Draksa. He dodged it easily with a graceful twist and a surge. His amusement filtered through the connection between them, and she sent, *Don't get cocky.* More amusement followed.

She called up another shield to block a force bolt as two of the invaders focused on Tanyith and one on her. The fourth, whom Fyre had clawed, was down and bleeding, and the fifth lay moaning from their attacks. She was preparing to counterattack when a shadow burst from her foe and she was forced to crouch behind her shield again.

When the tentacles reached around it and grasped her,

Cali panicked. She tried to yell the command word for her shield charm, but one of the strands of shadow magic covered her mouth and rendered her mute. She'd never heard of magic shaped into such a form and for a few moments, she wasn't able to believe it was happening. The tendrils lifted her off her feet, and she struggled against them with no success. Below, the duo pressured Tanyith and forced him to retreat so he couldn't help her.

Frye hurtled from above with an angry screech and clawed at the magical arms, but they vanished under his touch to be replaced by new ones almost instantaneously. They squeezed and she screamed against the one in her mouth. The enemy they'd knocked to the ground had found his feet and now fired blasts at the Draksa in an effort to drive him off. She looked through the stars in her vision at the man who slowly choked the breath out of her.

The arrogant grin on his face released a surge of rage through her, from the tips of her toes to the top of her head. *Oh, hell no. There's no way I'll go out like this.* She locked every thought in her brain into sections and sealed them off with caution tape until only the enemy and her power remained. Then, she released her restraint.

Magical fire exploded out of her, consumed the shadow tentacles, and traveled along them to her enemy. He attempted to shield but the flames seared through his defense and in an instant, he was simply no longer there. She fell and without conscious thought, caught herself with force magic to slow her descent and touched the ground with no more impact than if she'd taken a step. Ahead, the two Atlanteans with Tanyith spun in alarm. She blasted the one on the right with force and catapulted him away, and her partner did the same with the man on the left. Fyre focused on the injured man who had made it to his feet and rejoined the fight and froze him into an icy statue.

The power suddenly drained out of her, and Cali staggered, then forced herself upright. Tanyith ran to her and touched her arm. "Are you okay?"

She shook her head to clear it. "Yeah. The one who had me—he's gone, right?"

He nodded and she took a deep breath. She'd never killed someone before and had never wanted to kill anyone —for any reason. Nausea surged within her, but the practical voice in the back of her mind came to her rescue. *If you'd waited any longer, he would have killed you. He had every chance to stop. It was his choice, not yours.*

She shook her head at the voice but knew it was right. She forced herself to speak clearly. "Call Barton to arrange for someone to pick these bastards up. We need to check on the Dragons." She sent a message to Fyre to ask him to look for trouble along the way but if it wasn't urgent, not to worry about it. She'd fight again if she needed to, but all things considered, she'd had more than enough action for one night.

CHAPTER THIRTY

Rion Grisham was deeply and truly upset. He couldn't recall a time when he had been so angry—ever. To have a random group of alien bastards attack his organization without provocation was infuriating.

He paced in his office, not yet able to speak. His three trusted lieutenants sat on the couch and waited for him to break the silence, and the two who had assisted Ozahl in the battle against the New Atlanteans stood guard outside his door. He was off-balance, unsure who to trust, and worst of all, uncertain as to how to respond.

"What happened to the bastards who weren't killed?" he snapped. "Some must have only been wounded, right?"

Colin Todd, his suit mussed from the work they'd all done during the event, was quick to answer. "Yes, several, and our people are tracking them now. It looks like all of them—injured or captured—are being moved to Polk."

The gang leader growled in annoyance at the mention of the Army base. Fort Polk was large, annoyingly distant, and essentially out of his reach unless he wanted to cash in every favor owed to him. "Then we need to nab some before they get there. Ozahl, make it happen." The mage nodded an acknowledgment.

Anger welled inside him again, and he forced himself to speak in a measured tone. "I want to know everything about this. I want to know who was behind it. I want to know how they got here. I want to know who they were. I want to know where their families live. I want to know where their children go to school. Do you hear me? I want to know everything."

Silence reigned for a few moments before the wizard spoke. "What do you plan to do, boss?"

Grisham gave a thin smile. "I will rip them to pieces in every single way possible."

The mage looked thoughtful, then said, "I'm behind that idea and I'll do whatever I can to make it happen. But they might not be the greatest threat to us right now."

Everyone in the room, including him, stared at the magical in their midst. "What?" he demanded, his tone low and fierce.

Ozahl sat straighter on the couch. "I said this might not be our greatest threat. Let me explain." He held his index finger up. "One, this wasn't a fight for territory. They couldn't hope to eliminate us all in a single night, so the intent was to make a show of force, not to create something that would last. Well, we sent them packing, and they'll need time to regroup and consolidate before they can attack us again."

Grisham nodded. That tracked with his own thoughts on the matter.

The other man raised a second finger. "Two, we still have our current enemies to consider. The Atlantean gang in town could easily see this as a moment of weakness and make a push to take what's ours. We need to guard against that, first and foremost. We have to get our presence back on the street, continue to target their dealers, and recruit replacements for those we lost."

Again, he nodded. His anger had begun to cool into logic, and the mage had valid points.

He raised a third finger. "Finally, we're running low on a number of things we really need—including chemicals for our own drug trade and, more importantly, anti-magic bullets. If we can get enough of those, rather than keeping them in reserve, we could use them to wipe out the Atlantean gang once and for all."

The Zatora leader laughed. "You might as well ask for the world on a plate. Those are really tightly controlled. It's not even that they're expensive. There's merely no one to buy them from."

The mage smiled. "But, with a little effort, maybe we can find somewhere to steal them from."

A matching expression spread slowly across Rion Grisham's face. "Tell me more about that."

It felt like ages since Usha had last walked the streets of New Atlantis. When the Empress had summoned her, she'd wracked her brain for something she might have done wrong to require a personal meeting. In the end, she hadn't been able to think of anything, so she was cautiously hopeful she wouldn't receive a dressing down and that a positive reason lay behind the summons.

She'd considered bringing Danna to introduce her but had decided it would be inappropriate at best and insulting to her ruler at worst. Instead, she'd arrived at the portal landing zone alone and wearing her finest dress, which shimmered in turquoise. A large pearl ring glimmered on each of her index fingers, and she wore a dozen bracelets of coral on her left arm and gold on her right. A simple shell necklace encircled her throat. She walked through the streets of the central dome, which were laid out on a plane that bisected the sphere into a top and a bottom. If she looked up, she peered into the ocean where sea creatures of every kind swam in abundance. *Humans think the stars are beautiful. They have no idea what true beauty really is.*

The Empress's palace stood in the exact center of the space, its high central spire visible from almost anywhere in the city. This part of New Atlantis was about fifteen miles in diameter, with more than enough territory for the city's well-to-do citizens to spread their living areas. The inner-circle nearest the palace was separated into nine equal sections, one for each of the allegedly noble families. Those on the rise or those whose wealth was built through generations and served to give them influence with the nine occupied the remainder of the residences in the central dome.

Usha shook her head and muttered a curse. Her own humble beginnings outside the dome were not something she wanted to think about. Even worse, she didn't want to consider what failure would mean—that she would be banished out there once again. Those thoughts kept her mind occupied during the long walk to the palace.

When she finally arrived, she was recognized and permitted to enter without challenge. *That's a positive sign.* Remaining in the Empress's good graces was the primary goal of her entire existence. The hallways were lavishly ornamented, decorated with coral and gems and gold and every other treasure the sea held. Left to her own devices, she would be content to simply stare at them for hours. But she had a purpose and it would not permit even a second's delay.

Once, she had come as a commoner. Now, she could walk through the building with her head held high, a successful champion and a favorite of the Empress herself. She entered the throne room and immediately after she crossed the threshold, fell to one knee with her gaze lowered and her head bowed. She waited in silence. The first time she'd done this, she'd had to wait for hours and had felt like every second was a victory celebration.

Now, she only had to wait for her ruler to dismiss her other servants. The Empress's melodious voice commanded her to rise and approach, and she complied. She halted at the base of the nine stairs that lead to the dais and looked at the woman she owed everything to.

The most important person in New Atlantis smiled at her. "Things are changing, Usha. It is time we reconsidered our approach. Fear not, though. You will be the architect of our victory, exactly as I promised."

Usha's heart swelled with gratitude, and her pleasure only increased as the woman who was her whole world revealed her plans for the upstart family, the Zatoras, and most especially, Caliste Leblanc and her friends.

CHAPTER THIRTY-ONE

Tanyith walked into one of the oldest locals' bars in New Orleans, Stan's Pub. Everything was old wood, polished by use and pride of ownership. The lighting fixtures were antique-looking lanterns hung from walls and posts that created strange shadows around the room. It was mostly full, which was unusual for one o'clock on a Friday night going into Saturday morning. By now, the party in most French Quarter establishments had moved onto the streets.

The crowd in Stan's was different, though. He'd never crossed the threshold before because it was a cop bar and in his former role as Atlantean gang member, he wouldn't have been welcome. *To put it mildly.* He noticed Barton's short black hair first, then the off-duty leather jacket he'd seen her wear before. The only empty seat at the long wooden bar was beside her, and he slid onto it.

"Hey. What's up?" The late-night text had been a surprise but since he had a distinct lack of claims on his time, he'd accepted her invitation without hesitation. *I'm gonna have to find a real job soon but for now, I might as well enjoy the freedom.*

She gestured at the bartender and a tall glass of beer and a short one of something translucent appeared before each of them. She lifted her shot and swiveled toward him. "Cheers." He shrugged, picked his own up and clinked it against hers, then drank it. The kamikaze burned the length of his throat, but he managed to avoid coughing by taking a gulp of his beer. Barton looked at him with a small smile and nodded. "I wanted to thank you for your part in the action the other night."

He shrugged. "It had to be done. I'm glad I was able to help."

The detective pointed at him and the finger wobbled slightly, which suggested that she might be a drink or two ahead of him. "You are not the person I thought you were."

That prompted a laugh. "Is that a bad thing?"

Barton shook her head. "It is not. In fact, I might even call it a good thing. I would have hated to have to throw you in jail. Your redhead girlfriend would wind up in far more trouble without you around, I think."

Tanyith sighed. "Let me be completely clear. Cali. Is not. My girlfriend. Even if the age difference didn't shut that down—and it absolutely does—there's no spark there."

She looked hard into his eyes as if the truth was hiding in the back of his skull. "Are you sure of that? You two seem very tight."

"She's a friend. A good friend, even. But nothing more. Now, or ever."

The woman leaned back and looked thoughtful. "Well,

then. That's good to know." She stopped talking but continued to stare.

Tanyith cleared his throat. "So…uh, Detective Barton, would you be interested in going out to dinner sometime?"

Her laugh was freer than anything he'd heard from her before. "If you plan to hang out with me, you should at least start calling me Kendra. You can practice that on our date."

———

At about that same moment on the other side of the Quarter, Cali and Zeb were closing up for the evening. They'd let the Drunken Dragons stay open later than usual, as the magicals in the city seemed to have weighty things on their mind that night. Conversations were more intense but less confrontational. There seemed to be a little less joy but a little more community. They'd both noticed it and neither had wanted to shatter the unique atmosphere. A few stragglers still sat and talked, but most of the end of shift tasks could be done around them.

She slid onto one of the high bar chairs to take a break, tilted her chin in Fyre's direction, and whispered, "Hit him." The dwarf snagged the bar gun and fired a stream of soda water at the Draksa but as usual, the creature went from apparent sleep to fully awake in an instant. He growled, snapped at the flow, and drank the fizzy liquid. They laughed at his antics, and he settled again but kept a wary eye on them.

"So, quite the week we've had," Zeb said,

Cali nodded. "It was. Let's spend the next one resting, what do you say?"

He chuckled darkly. "Somehow, I don't think that's our decision to make."

Her gaze distant, she drummed her fingers on the bar. "Here's the thing about that. I'm actually kind of tired of being acted against instead of doing the acting."

The dwarf climbed into his own chair, lit his pipe, and took a deep pull. He blew smoke rings toward the Draksa, who steadfastly refused to notice. "That's understandable." He pointed the mouthpiece of the pipe at her. "You could spend more time at the library. That would be action of a sort."

"You are a sad, sad man who lacks vision." Her smile ensured he'd know she was teasing. "I thought about what my parents might have been doing in their lair. The more I consider it, the more it seems as if they were working against the gangs. Exactly like we are."

He nodded. "Agreed. And taking action brought them the wrong kind of attention."

"Very true. But that doesn't mean I would have the same result. I could succeed where they didn't. Plus, I have to understand what the deal is with Atreo and I have to find out how to decode those books. Add that to the urgent need to find out more about the bastards who sent a freaking Kraken to destroy the city, and there's really only one possible path forward."

Zeb straightened and stared at her, evidently realizing what she was planning. "Are you really sure you want to do that? There's getting closer to the fire and then there's jumping into it with both feet. This would definitely be the latter."

Cali nodded. "If I allow them to keep chipping away at me, I'll wind up exactly like my parents. I can't let that happen so I have to do it."

He shrugged. "If you have to, you have to." He laughed and shook his head. "Look out New Atlantis. Cali Leblanc is coming to town."

Cali, Fyre and her friends are heading to New Atlantis to investigate her legacy. But problems are still on the horizon back home in New Orleans. Join them as their adventure continues in *Bermuda Triangle Blues.*

If you enjoyed this book, you may also enjoy the first series from T.R. Cameron, also set in the Oriceran Universe. The Federal Agents of Magic series begins with Magic Ops and it's available now at Amazon and through Kindle Unlimited.

FBI Agent Diana Sheen is an agent with a secret...

...She carries a badge and a troll, along with a little magic.

But her Most Wanted List is going to take a little extra effort.

She'll have to embrace her powers and up her game to take down new threats,

Not to mention deal with the troll that's adopted her.

All signs point to a serious threat lurking just beyond sight, pulling the strings to put the forces of good in harm's way.

Magic or mundane, you break the law, and Diana's gonna find you, tag you and bring you in. Watch out magical baddies, this agent can level the playing field.

It's all in a day's work for the newest Federal Agent of Magic.

Available now at Amazon and through Kindle Unlimited

Thank you for reading the third book in the Scions of Magic series! I have to say, that while this one was an absolute challenge for some reason to write, I feel like the story it tells is deeply engaging. I'm really coming to love Cali, Fyre, and the rest. Plus, it's awesome to get more of Nylotte. As other life pressures worked on me during this time, the book really was a refuge. I am so grateful for the opportunity to share stories with you.

The unwavering support and ideas from Martha and Michael have been fantastic. Getting the keys to their world to build out the Atlantean culture is a real mark of trust, one that hopefully I'm justifying, and has been fantastic fun. In book four we'll get a better look at the underwater city, as the second main story arc begins. The initial plan was for three sets of three, but right now I feel like there's enough stories in Cali and her comrades for more than that. Guess that will be up to whether y'all want more!

So much has happened since the last author notes!

20booksto50k was amazing, as always. Being around that many indie and hybrid authors, all united in the common goal of telling great stories for great fans, is a soul-enriching experience. If I knew everything there was to know about that stuff (which I don't, for sure), I would still go for the energy. It refills my own pool of writing power.

I finished Outer Worlds. It was alright, not the best ever. Skyrim and Fallout 4 still hold those titles for me. I managed to get the kid, finally, to watch Star Wars: A New Hope. Positive response. We'll be doing Vader Immortal in VR over the holiday break, which is something big to look forward to.

Still busy, way busy, too busy. My day job gives me a little extra time off during December, and I'm really looking forward to spending them with my child, playing board games (Carcassone is the current fave, and looking forward to getting Catan Jr. as well), video games (Death Stranding is the weirdest game I've ever seen), and seeing the last of the most recent Star Wars trilogy.

I'm writing this in the center seat of a plane. My family and I are headed for Disney World and Universal studios. I promised the kid that we'd do a "big" trip every four years, and the last one was four years ago, so it was time to make good on it. My emotions around it are weird. I'm very excited for the intense, responsibility-free time we'll share. But I'm also well aware that this is the last time we'll do something like this before she's almost a teenager, which means most of the kid-stuff joys won't be appealing anymore. No regrets, just, I guess, a moment of passage.

I'm beyond excited for season four of The Expanse, but have to finish getting through the earlier seasons a third time to prepare. If you're a sci-fi fan and you're not watching (and reading), take my word for it, you should, you'll love it.

As we head into the end of the year and the finish of the decade, the temptation is to look back and judge, or look forward and hope. My personal goal is to try to embrace the moment as much as I can. I'm not good at that, but hey, no time like the present to improve!

Until next time, Joys upon joys to you and yours – so may it be.

PS: If you'd like to chat with me, here's the place. I check in daily or more:

https://www.facebook.com/AuthorTRCameron.

For more info on my books, and to join my reader's group, please visit https://www.trcameron.com.

Stay up to date on new releases and fan pricing by signing up for my newsletter. CLICK HERE TO JOIN.

Or visit: www.trcameron.com/Oriceran to sign up.

If you enjoyed this book, please consider leaving a review.

Thanks!

Have you ever met someone and with everything you learn about them your admiration grows, and then like a fun twist in a really good book you find out they have a layer of sass as well? That's Kelly O'Donnell.

I've known Kelly since The Leira Chronicles began back in the summer of 2017, which in my world is forever! Even then she was able to keep me straight with plot points because after book six of anything I start to forget. What can I say?

And I like to put a lot of details in my books. On top of that I took a break from The Leira Chronicles for over a year and now I'm back writing another adventure. It's been hard to remember what Eireka's new husband's name is or which arm Perrom lost, or what that society of witches was called and a million other details. I'll stop there in case anyone is now giving me a YTT Aloha for spoilers I was about to say... Never mind.

The point is lately I have been peppering Kelly with endless questions and she knows a lot of them off the top of her head and when she doesn't, she knows how to find them – and it's all done with grace and joy.

Even better, I had a chance to spend some time with her in Scotland and I realized there is a finely tuned snarky sense of humor under that layer of kindness that is my idea of human perfection. Imagine being able to be funny and never at someone else's expense. That's Kelly O'Donnell. I don't know if this is true, but I picture her on a Harley on her way to a bake sale and she rescues a pit bull on the side of the road along the way. Probably all fiction, but I wouldn't be surprised...

1. What turns you on?

Broad shoulders and a sense of humor.

2. What turns you off?

Liars.

3. Who do you most admire? Why?

Any first responder/ military. They are the ones running into the situations and standing on that line saying 'not today, asshole, not today.'

4. What profession other than your own would you like to attempt?

Sniper 12

5. What profession would you not like to do?

Anything in retail.

6. If heaven exists, what would you like to hear God say when you arrive at the pearly gates?

We gave you a free pass in, but damn, child, we had to think about it.

7. What is your favorite movie?

Lord of the Rings (all of them)

8. Who is your favorite character and from what book by which author?

Wow, that's a tough one. I like so many of them for various reasons... Gonna have to go with Major Xi Bao from the Metal Legion series by C.H. Gideon.

9. What is something most people do not know about you?

I'm a homebody.

10. What do you look forward to most in the new year?

Seeing what this crazy fabulous life has in store for me. Good or bad, life's an adventure and I for one enjoy that I'm still here for it.

11. What's your favorite non-LMBPN series you've done? What's your favorite series inside LMBPN?

Not an author so as a reader I find myself rereading Traders Tales by Nathan Lowell just about once a quarter. As for a LMBPN series, I really enjoy any and all of the Zoo universe.

OTHER SERIES IN THE ORICERAN
UNIVERSE:

THE DANIEL CODEX SERIES
I FEAR NO EVIL
THE UNBELIEVABLE MR. BROWNSTONE
ALISON BROWNSTONE
SCHOOL OF NECESSARY MAGIC
SCHOOL OF NECESSARY MAGIC: RAINE CAMPBELL
FEDERAL AGENTS OF MAGIC
SCIONS OF MAGIC
THE LEIRA CHRONICLES
REWRITING JUSTICE
THE KACY CHRONICLES
MIDWEST MAGIC CHRONICLES
SOUL STONE MAGE
THE FAIRHAVEN CHRONICLES

OTHER BOOKS BY JUDITH BERENS

CONNECT WITH THE AUTHORS

TR Cameron Social

Website: www.trcameron.com

Facebook: https://www.
facebook.com/AuthorTRCameron

Martha Carr Social

Website: http://www.marthacarr.com

Facebook: https://www.facebook.com/
groups/MarthaCarrFans/

Michael Anderle Social

Michael Anderle Social
Website:
http://www.lmbpn.com

Email List:
http://lmbpn.com/email/

Facebook Here: https://www.facebook.com/TheKurtherianGambitBooks/

Made in the USA
Las Vegas, NV
15 March 2023

69127466R00166